"What do you wan̶̶̶̶̶̶̶̶̶̶̶̶̶̶̶̶̶̶̶̶ on the words.

"We're going to get married."

The ground swayed beneath her feet and the trees closed in as she struggled to retain control of her swirling senses.

"Married?" She could barely whisper.

"Yup." He rolled back further on his heels and rested his hands on his hips. "Haven't got time to run the house. Too busy with the ranch. I need a woman."

Her cheeks sagged and she felt the blood drain away. She was sure her face had lost all its color. Then red-hot anger raced upward, burning her cheeks and flooding her brain with such force that words rushed from her mouth. "You think you can just grab a girl and plunk her on your horse and race off with her and announce you're going to get married? Just who do you think you are anyway, Mr. Brewster Johnson? This is a free country. Slavery is not allowed." Her mouth was so dry she choked and was forced to stop and swallow hard. The infuriating man stood there scowling at her, his eyes shadowed by his hat, his mouth tight. She glowered at him. "If you're so all-fired anxious to get married, why don't you court a girl like anyone else?"

He dropped his hands to his sides and hunched forward. "Wouldn't work."

"How do you know?" She spat the words at him. "Have you tried?"

"I just know." His jaw tightened and his hands closed into fists.

LINDA FORD draws on her own experiences in the Canadian Rockies to paint this wonderful adventure in romance and faith. Linda lives in Alberta, Canada, with her family and is a member of the Alberta Romance Writers Association.

Books by Linda Ford

HEARTSONG PRESENTS
HP240—The Sun Still Shines

Unchained
Hearts

Linda Ford

Heartsong Presents

To Sharon, who was there from the beginning. Thank you for your never-failing support and encouragement. Your friendship makes my life richer. God bless.

A note from the author:
I love to hear from my readers! You may write to me at the following address: **Linda Ford**
Author Relations
PO Box 719
Uhrichsville, OH 44683

ISBN 1-57748-282-4

UNCHAINED HEARTS

All of the characters and events in this book are fictitious.
Any resemblance to actual persons, living or dead, or to
actual events is purely coincidental.

Cover illustration by Kathy Arbuckle.

PRINTED IN THE U.S.A.

one

1882
The Northwest Territories of Canada

Abby turned her face heavenward and laughed. She liked the way her voice drifted across the waving grass. She still couldn't get over the breadth of the sky, which seemed to spread from one week to the next, nor the beauty of the Rocky Mountains, jagged and mysterious against the western horizon. While Andrew was away overnight checking on some brood mares that he hoped to add to their herd, she was going to allow herself some time to explore this inviting countryside. Longing to run in wild abandon across the vast meadow, she hugged herself, and her heart bounced like the grass dancing in the wind.

Andrew had promised her a trip to town after he returned. She had to admit that living twenty miles from the nearest settlement took a little getting used to and she longed to check for letters from home and have a visit with Sarah. How blessed she was that God had provided a friend like Sarah in this new land.

First though, she would take the laundry off the line.

Scooping up the empty wicker basket, still yellow in its newness, she sauntered across the yard, smiling as her eyes continued to drink in the scenery. A thicket of aspens sheltered the house and yard, but from where the clothesline stood on the edge of the slope, she could enjoy an unobstructed view of the hills drifting into the blue distance and disappearing in the shadow of the jagged skyline to the west.

The sheets snapped in the brisk wind and Abby shook her head, letting the warm breeze sift through her hair and whisper in her ear. There was no one to notice that most of the hairpins had fallen out, letting her hair escape the bun she had wound up tightly a short time before. Another pin fell to the ground and her hair whipped against her cheek. She bent and retrieved the bit of hardware, and dropped it into her pocket. It was useless to try to put the bun back in place. Her hair was such a nuisance—thick and wiry, with enough curl to make it impossible to control. If there were one thing she could change about herself, it would be her hair. She had often wished for smooth hair, and plain brown rather than the copper color of an old penny.

As she grabbed the clothesline and pulled off the pegs, she forgot the vexation of unruly hair. The sun was so bright she couldn't help but hum along with the wind.

The breeze caught the sheet, blowing it against her body. Straining against the white waves, she laughed as the material skipped free. Suddenly, her arms were pressed to her side. Gasping, she looked down to see black-sleeved arms wrapped around her. Her heart kicked against her ribs and she screamed. The arms tightened against her, jerking her off her feet. She choked and the wind sucked away her screams. Feeling like a fist had slammed into her heart, she gasped for air, her mind racing with frightening images. She steeled her racing thoughts. Was someone playing a cruel joke? Her throat clamped shut as terror flooded through her.

Her captor turned and hauled her away from the edge of the hill, jolting her like an awkward sack of corn. She flailed her feet against her assailant's legs, her heels thudding against solid bone, but the man didn't slow. She squirmed upward, desperate to escape the viselike grip that pressed her into his warm, solid chest. Uncoiling every scrap of strength, she flung herself backward. Her head connected with a sharp chin and she felt a puff of satisfaction at the grunt from her captor.

Her efforts to break his grasp increased, but his hold tightened. A low growl rose from her throat—a sound totally unfamiliar to her. With her mouth now as dry as old grass, she continued to twist against the steel-like arms. His grasp tightened further.

Gritting her teeth, she stiffened her shoulders and strained upward against his arms. His grip tightened until she could barely breathe. A great knot seemed to have lodged in her chest, the pain shooting blinding spears to her mind. She was wallowing in the pain, the tightness, the terror.

Unaffected by her weight or her struggling, her captor continued his jerky journey. His fists, digging into the soft spot just below her breastbone, felt like heavy iron weights squeezing the air out and compressing her lungs. Every time she released a breath, the fists pushed in further until she was suffocating.

Twisting her arms, trying to free them from the mighty trap, only caused the pressure to increase. If only she could wrench a hand free. If she could manage to jab an elbow into his ribs. . .

She panted, her lungs screaming for release, her heart thundering for oxygen, her brain knee-deep in flashing stars.

The world blackened and tilted. From the edges of her mind, she was aware they had entered the shelter of the trees. A tall, black horse lifted its head to watch them. Then the arms loosened and she sucked in air, gasping it into her starving lungs. The darkness receded and the world righted itself. Feeling him strain to one side as he reached for the reins, she squeezed her eyes into slits. She had to get away. *Escape.* The word blazed through her brain. The best time would be just as he reached out to flip the reins over the neck of the horse. She would not miss her chance. She breathed a silent prayer. *God, help me.* Coiling her muscles, she counted the seconds. *One, two, three. Now.* She flung her muscles into action, throwing her hands upward, heaving against the arm that girdled her to his chest, her feet searching for traction.

A muffled grunt echoed above her head and his arm tightened, swinging her off her feet. She was heaved upward and thrown into the saddle in front of him, molded to his legs and chest.

At five feet six, Abby did not consider herself tiny. She wouldn't have thought anyone could swing her into the air like that. Her helplessness against such strength seared her thoughts. Terror, red-hot and suffocating, flashed through her mind, erupting in shrill panic-laced screeches that came out the top of her head, rising, rising, rising until she was consumed by them.

A hand clamped over her mouth, and her terror increased as her lungs again fought for air. She twisted her head back and forth. Drawing back her lips, she buried her teeth in his palm. He grunted and cupped his hand to escape her bite, but his fingers continued to dig into her cheeks. He pressed her head to the hollow of his neck and dug his chin into the top of her head, making it impossible for her to move her head. She squirmed, twisting her torso, scraping across the rough horse-hide. The horse pranced nervously but her captor held the reins firmly, completely in control, and the horse calmed. The man crushed her to him harshly, almost raising her off the saddle. She pounded the horse with her heels. Without a word, the man took his feet from the stirrups and covered her legs with his own so it was impossible to move her legs. His silence was unsettling. It triggered tremors in her limbs and she clenched her teeth to keep them from chattering.

Firmly encased in his grasp, all she could move were her eyeballs. Finding no outlet in shrill screeches or frenzied physical acts, her terror gelled into something deeper and more awesome, coagulating into a solid mass settling into her stomach. She had always thought one's heart turned to stone in times of shock, but now she knew it reverberated with depths she could never have imagined. Each heartbeat felt like a tear inside her ribs, ripping her heart to shreds. She had no idea what her captor planned but her imagination skittered across the likelihood of what lay ahead. Would he rape her and leave her to perish, lost and alone in the thick forest? Would he do the deed and murder her? Who was her captor? Was he an Indian? She'd heard of the tortures of some of the

Indian tribes. She squeezed her eyes shut, trying to ease the pounding behind them. Then another, even more terrible idea emerged. She had heard the words whispered behind hands and even then had recoiled in disgust. *White slavery. Oh, God!* she silently cried. *God, my shield and defender. You promised you would never leave me nor forsake me.*

The flashes of light inside her head faded. She was able to suck air past her pounding heart, and fill her lungs.

The arm of her captor relaxed slightly, allowing her to settle in the cramped saddle she shared with him. An evil man should have a repugnant smell, but this man bore the smell of pine needles and freshly cut hay. Odd how her senses seemed so sharp. Was it fear, or lack of air that made them so, she wondered. Every sensation was magnified—the scratch of the horse's mane against her hands, the taste of salt on her lips, the grunt of the horse as its hooves struck the ground, the rise and fall of the chest at her back.

"If you won't scream, I'll take my hand from your mouth."

They were the first words he had spoken. His voice was gravelly and low, like water running over a rough streambed.

She considered his offer. Why should she agree? She must use every means at her disposal to escape. On the other hand, they had been riding through thick pine forest long enough for her to know that the chances of anyone hearing her screams were remote. Unless she were to count the deer and other wild animals. Yet something deep within her knew that if she gave her promise—even by silent consent—she would feel honor bound to keep it, even in this situation. She heard her father's gentle voice telling her, "Let your yes be yes, and your no, no." The habit of speaking honestly was too deeply ingrained for her to be able to ignore it. Barely able to move her head, she managed a slight nod and he slowly lifted his hand.

Her mouth felt wooden and she stretched her cheeks and grimaced.

He let his arms slide down her body, freeing her. She flexed her fingers to restore circulation and rubbed her mouth.

"What are you going to do to me?" Her lips were wooden.

"I mean you no harm." Again the low voice, almost a growl.

Twisting in the saddle, she tried to catch a glimpse of her captor, but he leaned forward, pressing her against the saddle horn.

"Don't turn around," he ordered, and by a touch of the reins turned the horse onto a narrow, almost invisible trail.

Was it just this morning she had waved good-bye to Andrew and laughed at the thought of a day to herself? She could remember congratulating herself on how perfect life was. In a matter of minutes, her life had cartwheeled into disaster. She choked back the bitterness rising in her throat.

The words *I will never leave you* drummed inside her heart. For a moment she resisted their message of assurance. Where was God now? But they echoed again and she allowed the thought to calm her as she recalled the little game Father had taught them.

"Hold up your fingers," he had told them. "Now use each one for a word." And he had marched his fingertip over their fanned fingers, at each saying a word "I—will—never—leave—you."

"Never forget it," he had admonished.

She tightened each digit against the palm of her hand as she forced herself to repeat the words over and over.

They rode slower, ducking under low branches. Once, he reached out to lift a heavy bough and they bent low to avoid it.

As the darkness of the thick woods increased, so did Abby's fear. It rose in her stomach and puckered her mouth like a long drink of sour milk. It rolled inside her belly on a wave of nausea and she gritted her teeth, as much to keep them from chattering as to quell the urge to vomit. She would not let him know how afraid she was.

Around her clenched teeth, she demanded, "If you mean me no harm, then take me back home."

She felt him shake his head, and for a minute she couldn't

control the rattle of her jaw. "Take me home," she pleaded. "I won't tell anyone." She had not seen his face. It would be impossible to identify him. She babbled the words, desperate for him to see this was to his advantage. But again, she felt the shake of his head.

"I'm not taking you home." The words vibrated along her spine, racing through her body like a fever.

"Let me go," she ground out, flailing her legs and arms like a flapping towel in the wind. The horse tossed his head and whinnied. A branch slapped her in the face and she whimpered. Again, he pressed his legs over hers and pinned her arms to her sides so she couldn't move.

"Settle down," he growled. "Just settle down."

"No," she panted. "I won't settle down. Let me go." Her words turned to a sob. "Please, let me go."

"I can't."

She stiffened, every nerve alert to his meaning. "Why? What are you going to do?"

He was picking his way through a thick tangle of trees and didn't answer. They broke into a small, sunless clearing, completely shrouded by tall pines. A fine-boned, black horse, matching the one they rode, was tethered at the far side. In a flash, Abby took in the details. The rolled-up bedroll and saddle on the ground, a piece of canvas draped over them. The saddlebags high in the trees beside two canteens. This had been his camp for at least two days, she guessed by the tripod over the dead ashes. He looked to be supplied for many days in the wilds.

"No." The moan came unbidden to her throat, and she struggled against his arms. "What are you going to do?" She was drowning in her own panic, and she felt her limbs go rubbery. "What do you want?"

The horse snorted and pawed the ground, restless to be free of its unpredictable burden. The man shifted in the saddle, and for a minute Abby thought he was going to step down without answering her. Then he grunted, a sound that might have been him clearing his throat.

If only he would get down first, she would have a few seconds to grab the reins and kick the horse into flight. If she could just get into the bush. . .

She stared at the mass of dark trees. The forest was thick and moody and she trembled at the thought of being lost in its gloom without provision or protection, but it was preferable to what lay ahead here. He must have guessed her thoughts, for he stiffened and his arm tightened painfully.

"We're gonna get down," he growled, and she heard and understood the warning note in his voice. "You aren't gonna try and run away or I'll have to tie you up." He paused and she waited, but they stayed seated in the saddle. "One more thing. When you see me, you better not scream."

She shook her head, wondering at his warning.

"Ready?"

Before she could nod, he swung his leg over and lifted her from the saddle. Gasping at the pressure against her rib cage, she was dragged off the horse and set on her feet. It was the longest she had ever been on the back of a horse and the inside of her legs screamed a protest. Her knees threatened to buckle. His arm steadied her until her rubbery limbs took her weight and then he stepped back.

She spun on her heel and stared at her captor.

Draped in a long, black slicker, he gave the impression of power and—she struggled for the right word—it wasn't evil she read in his face, though she had no doubt his intentions were just that. It was more a sense of warning, a belligerence accented by the dark scowl on his face. His face might have been called handsome apart from the brooding scowl and a scar puckering his left cheek. He turned his head slightly and under the shadow of the battered, black cowboy hat that hid all of his hair but a thick black fringe at the nape, she caught a glimpse of dark, hazel eyes, veiled and unfathomable. It was hard to guess his age—somewhere in his late thirties, she thought, though it could be the hardness in his face that made him look that old.

"Who are you?" she demanded in a strong, clear voice that revealed none of the inner terror making her arms feel extra long and her hands seem detached from her body. Her feet had the same not-quite-there feeling. "What do you want?"

He settled back on his heels, his stance wide, his arms loose at his sides, yet she sensed his steady gaze and knew he watched her with the sharpness of a hawk. "My name is Brewster Johnson." He nodded. "And you are Abigail Landor."

Her eyes widened. "How do you know my name?" At the same time, her mind was searching for a tidbit tucked away. She knew she had heard that name before. Suddenly she remembered Sarah's words.

"You have a neighbor west of you," she had said. "A dark, brooding man. He rides into town with his hat pulled low, gathers up what he needs and rides out again, as silent as the morning mist."

What else had Sarah said about him?

Abby remembered thinking at the time that he lived too far away to be making social calls. A shudder wriggled up her spine. One could hardly call this a social visit.

"I know lots about you. You have a brother, Andrew, and you arrived here a few months ago."

"He's my twin brother." It seemed important he get the facts right.

"Yup. Know that too."

"What do you want?" She almost choked on the words.

"We're going to get married."

The ground swayed beneath her feet and the trees closed in as she struggled to retain control of her swirling senses.

"Married?" She could barely whisper.

"Yup." He rolled back further on his heels and rested his hands on his hips. "Haven't got time to run the house. Too busy with the ranch. I need a woman."

Her cheeks sagged and she felt the blood drain away. She

was sure her face had lost all its color. Then red-hot anger raced upward, burning her cheeks and flooding her brain with such force that words rushed from her mouth. "You think you can just grab a girl and plunk her on your horse and race off with her and announce you're going to get married? Just who do you think you are anyway, Mr. Brewster Johnson? This is a free country. Slavery is not allowed." Her mouth was so dry she choked and was forced to stop and swallow hard. The infuriating man stood there scowling at her, his eyes shadowed by his hat, his mouth tight. She glowered at him. "If you're so all-fired anxious to get married, why don't you court a girl like anyone else?"

He dropped his hands to his sides and hunched forward. "Wouldn't work."

"How do you know?" She spat the words at him. "Have you tried?"

"I just know." His jaw tightened and his hands closed into fists.

"How can you be so all-fired sure?" She saw him tense. Not knowing what to expect if she angered him, she backed away, her insides fluttering as her gaze darted around the clearing. There was no place to run.

"You see me," he growled. "I'm ugly. What girl in her right mind is gonna take a second look at me?" His fingers touched the scar on his cheek.

She took a step back. She didn't know what she had expected, but not that. Ugly? No, she wouldn't call him ugly, at least not his features. What made him unattractive was the way he scowled. Her anger mounted. She could feel it spark in her eyes. "Mr. Johnson, it is not your face I find objectionable. It is your high-handed attitude. You can't just grab a girl and force her to marry you."

He laughed. At least, she supposed she could call his snort of derision a laugh. "Maybe I'll forget the preacher bit and just take you to my cabin. We don't need to be married for you to cook and clean."

"You—that's not—" She paused and swallowed. "You can't make me marry you." She sought for control. How dare this man think he could choose a wife this way? Was he crazy? Her heart ticking in her throat, she gathered up her skirts and dashed for the deep woods, only steps to her right. Being lost in the woods was preferable to whatever this lunatic had planned.

Behind her, she heard his angry growl, and then his thudding footsteps. She increased her pace. Parting the bushes, she dived under the branches, jerking her skirts as they caught. Keeping low, she scooted through the thicket until the forest closed around her. For a ragged moment, she forced herself to remain still as she gathered air into her aching lungs and calmed her breathing.

Twigs snapped and branches cracked as he thundered after her. Knowing his noise would hide the sounds of her escape, she grabbed her skirt and pulled it between her legs, tucking it firmly into her waistband. Dropping to her hands and knees, she scurried deeper into the forest, pushing her way into thick growth, wriggling under the low branches and tangled brush. The underbrush scratched her face, but she pressed on, deeper and deeper into the protection of the thicket. When she was sure she was hidden from view, she huddled into a ball and held her breath, listening. The forest was silent. A beetle scurried across her arm and she choked back a sob. A seed pod snapped, loud as a drum beat in the damp silence. She didn't dare take a breath. It would signal her hiding place like a red flag. She forced herself to ignore the burning in her lungs. A branch snapped so close she could feel the sound. Rustling sounds of boots on a leafy forest floor moved past her and faded. She dropped her head to her knees and drew a shaky breath, letting the air seep into her famished lungs.

Andrew, she silently called, *I need you.* It wasn't unusual for them to be able to communicate without using words and she prayed this would be one of those times. Even as she thought it, though, she knew he was too far away to help. He wouldn't even know she was gone until tomorrow. Hot tears puddled on the back of her hands. How long would she have to huddle here until it was safe to make her way home? How long would he wait for her to crawl out? The forest floor was cold and damp, and she shivered.

Again and again she repeated the words, *I will never leave you nor forsake you.* Another verse Father had taught them tacked itself to her litany. *What time I am afraid, I will trust in thee. I will not fear what flesh can do unto me.*

No matter what happened, she had the assurance that God would be with her to help. Her breathing deepened. Was Sarah praying for her now?

She remembered her pleasure the first time she met Sarah. Sarah had been helping her husband, Tom, in the general mercantile store in the fledgling settlement of Pine Creek. The plain, young woman had a spark that drew Abby's interest. Similar in age, there had been an immediate sense of kinship between them despite the infant Sarah carried in one arm. It didn't take either of them long to discover that they shared the same faith in God and excitement in this wonderful, new land. When Sarah had suggested they pray for each other, Abby had readily agreed.

She drew strength from the thought that Sarah would be upholding her before God, and centered her thoughts on Andrew. He wouldn't know what to think when he returned and found her missing. If only he wouldn't blame himself. But she knew he would. He had always been protective of her, just as she felt it was her responsibility to care for him. It came of being motherless since they were three. Father had been there, quiet and loving, but she and Andrew had given each other the affection and understanding their mother would have provided if she had lived. Being twins only strengthened the bond between them. They were like matching bookends.

They even shared the same dreams. For three years, stirred by the stories Cousin James had read in letters from a friend in Canada, they had worked and saved and planned for this move. And now, just months after they had found the ideal spot in the foothills west of Fort Calgary, this madman had ridden in to ruin their lives.

What would Father say when he heard of her disappearance? Closing her eyes, she thought of his pain. Father had planned to come with them, but as the time drew near, he had gently said he didn't think he could stand to be so far from Mama. He still went to her grave every week. It was the only thing that marred their happiness, but Abby knew he was right. He would never have been content leaving Mama behind.

But if something were to happen to Abby, she feared it would drive him to an early grave.

Her jaw tensed as she huddled in the damp forest. How could this madman think he could force her into marriage? Why, it was barbaric! Had he escaped from the Dark Ages? She shuddered and drew her knees closer to her chest, promising herself she would perish in the gloom of the forest before she would let him find her.

Poor Andrew. He would never find her hiding place either.

A spasm clawed at her neck and ran its sharp talons into the small of her back. She stiffened against the pain. How long could she stay in this position? Already she could feel pins and needles jabbing in her thighs. She shifted her weight to her right, but even that little bit of movement set the leaves dancing and jingling. She forced herself to remain motionless, letting her breath slide silently in and out. The stillness was alive with normal forest sounds—birds gossiping in the foliage, pine needles whispering in the treetops, wind sighing through the branches. She strained to catch a sound that would provide a clue to the man's whereabouts. Her ears hummed from listening but she could not detect anything out of place.

The talons in her back dug deeper. Her legs twitched and she grasped them tighter to keep them from jerking outward. How long had she been hiding? She tried to measure the day but it had occurred in flashes of fear and tension rather than in minutes and hours. They had ridden far enough to penetrate the pine forest. She estimated that would have taken at least an hour, probably longer. She had been huddled here long enough to make her limbs cramp. Probably another hour. It was hard to tell by the light because it would be dull under the trees even at midday, but she guessed it had to be late afternoon. She hadn't heard a sound from her captor in a long time. Every nerve in her body cried for relief, but she kept her head lowered to her knees, her heart surging against her chest, as she contemplated the noise she would make if she moved. Finally, she couldn't stand the discomfort any longer. Moving with the speed of Old Lady Sparks, who was so crippled she could barely inch her way across the street, she lifted her head.

Her heart almost exploded. A scream rose in her throat, unfolded in the air like a thin piece of paper, then tucked into a moan and dropped to the pit of her stomach where it lay like a cold rock.

Like some monstrous bat, silent and unnatural, her captor leaned against a tree, his black slicker draped at his sides. His eyes, guarded by his hat, didn't so much as twitch. His arms were crossed over his chest. One scuffed, worn, black boot rested against the instep of the other as he waited, as still as a shadow.

two

He uncoiled with deliberate slowness.

"I could track a mouse up a tree in a rainstorm." His voice was deep and ominous.

She tried to swallow but her throat closed up. She was paralyzed before his unblinking watchfulness—fearing he would strike; not knowing when. Her heart turned cold. This staring, unmoving stranger was more frightening than when he had crushed her in his grip.

"You can come out or I can drag you out."

Her fear ignited, jolting her into action.

She staggered upright, gritting her teeth as daggers stabbed through her feet and legs. It took a full minute before she could straighten herself completely. She looked him squarely in the eye. She didn't say a thing. She didn't need to. Her clenched jaw and the defiance that made her eyes feel brittle were all that were necessary. He may have prevented her escape, but he didn't have her beaten. No amount of force or threats or torture could make her give in to his demands. She would never give in!

His eyes darkened to match the green of the pine needles behind him and she knew he had read her message and understood it. Just as surely, she understood his answering certainty.

"Back to camp," he ordered.

She glanced around her. It all looked the same but she stepped to the right.

He grabbed her upper arm and tugged her to the left. "Wrong way," he growled. She lurched after him, dragged along by his hand. His grasp was firm enough to warn her that if she tried to run, he would jerk her to a stop before she could go half a step, but she had no intention of running again. Not right now. The darkness of the forest was rapidly closing in on them. She could hardly see where to put her feet. And with the deepening gloom came penetrating cold. No, she would sit by a fire and get warm before she made another attempt.

They burst into the clearing. Black shapes loomed across the patch of pine needles. A shudder shook her body. He felt it.

"I'll light the fire soon as I tie you up."

She tried to wrench free. "No." It was bad enough to be kidnapped, and held in this black hole in the forest. She couldn't bear being tied up as well.

"I warned you." He dragged her toward the horse. She dug in her heels but he continued on, almost jerking her off her feet. As he uncoiled a rope from the saddle, she twisted her hands and wriggled her wrists like a snake squirming out of a hole. His thumb burrowed deep into her flesh and his grip tightened until her bones ached from the pressure.

"Please, don't tie me up." Her exertions had left her breathless and her voice whispery.

"I can't spend all my time hunting you down." Without looking at her, he pulled her hands together in front of her, and wrapped the rope around each wrist, the coils digging into her tender flesh. With a flick of his wrists, he knotted the rope between her hands and pulled both ends into his palm, leaving five feet of double-stranded rope between them. Although he had secured her wrists well, he had left her hands loose enough to allow movement.

"You can't do this." Clamping her jaw, she flung herself backwards. The rope tightened around his fist and his slicker flapped in the shadows. Her teeth rattled as the rope snapped taut.

"Settle down," he growled. "Follow me. I'm going to build a fire and make something to eat."

He couldn't make her settle down. She'd fight him at every opportunity. She tugged at the rope, forcing him to keep his fist tight around his end. She dipped to her right, intending to fling herself on the ground. What would he do if she lay there and refused to move? Her throat tightened as she remembered his plans for her, and she straightened, knowing she would be at a terrible disadvantage flat on the ground. And as long as he was expecting her to try to break loose, she realized, he would not slacken his hold on the rope. If she could get him to let down his guard, perhaps he would forget about clutching the ends. Trotting after him, she decided to wait her chance.

Settle down. Silently, she repeated his order, forcing her fear back, back, back until it was like a sleeping bear in a cave. She filled her lungs and held her breath for the count of two and let it ease past her clenched teeth. A fragile calm seeped through her limbs.

Wood was already laid for a fire and it started instantly when he put a match to it. "We need more wood." He strode toward the forest with Abby scurrying in his wake. "Hold out your arms. I'll fill them."

Separated by the slender strands of rope, she stared at him as he bent to pick up deadwood. Anger choked at the back of her throat and her eyes were tight with fear, but she blinked back her emotions and waited as he piled several small pieces of wood in her arms. Perhaps her silent consent would do what she could not trust her voice to do—convince him she was prepared to cooperate. The rough bark burned at the tender flesh of her inner arms and the rope tightened around her wrists as she strained to hold the weight of her burden close to her body so the coils wouldn't bite so harshly. He bent to pick up wood to fill his own arms. As he straightened, she gritted her teeth to keep from showing her discomfort. She was aware of his scrutiny but it was too dark to be able to make out the expression in his eyes. Did he have any idea how painful it was for her to have her wrists bound? She bit her bottom lip.

They piled the wood close to the fire. Brewster bent and

pulled a blackened cast-iron pot out of the saddlebags.

"Can I help?" she croaked.

"Can you make mush?"

"Of course."

He poured a handful of meal into water and set the pot on a rock near the fire, then handed her a spoon. She stirred until the gruel thickened, all the time keeping her head turned away so he wouldn't see the desperate fear making her limbs feel like string. If only she could poison the pot. She'd gladly die to escape what lay ahead.

Turning back to the saddlebag, he poured a scoop of coffee into a blue enamel coffeepot and hung it over the fire, then opened a can of baked beans and set it between two rocks near the flames. The aromas blended and wrapped around her, making her forget the dark shadows sucking the light from the clearing, and the rope that bound her wrists. As the smell of beans, cornmeal, and coffee rose on the thin twist of smoke, she sank to the ground.

Filling a battered tin plate, he handed it to her. She felt resentment flare in her eyes and lowered them, waiting until he turned back to the fire before she pulled the plate to her chin and shoveled the food into her mouth with short jerky movements. When she finished, he took her plate and handed her a cup of coffee. She savored its warmth. As comfort spread outward to her limbs, she allowed herself to relax. Out of the corner of her eye, she watched Brewster cleaning his plate. The rope tying her to him rested in his fist.

Taking a deep breath, she turned to him. "Do you live close by?" She hoped he would enjoy talking about his place as much as she and Andrew did about theirs.

"Up the mountain some," he grunted, not bothering to lift his head.

"What sort of place do you have?" *Keep pressing him to talk. Get him to let down his guard.*

"Just a small place."

"A log house?"

"Of sorts."

He was as closemouthed as he was unsmiling. "You originally from around here?"

"Nope."

"Where are you from?"

"No place in particular."

She stared at him. His expression never relaxed. The lines in his face were as deeply engraved as the scar. His left side was to her and she studied the scar. Whatever had happened, it was not a clean cut. The edges were puckered like he had caught his cheek on something sharp. It was an old injury, she guessed, for the scar was silvery white and almost invisible except when he turned and the light caught it as it did now. He met her gaze with dark, motionless eyes. She knew he had seen her studying his scar and she read the challenge in his eyes.

Blinking before his stare, yet determined not to be intimidated, she asked, "What happened?"

He turned away and ducked his head, hiding his face under the brim of his hat. "Got cut." His voice was hard as rock.

It seemed the more she asked him questions, the more he tightened up. She lighted on another topic. "Do you have family? Parents, brothers, sisters?"

"None." His voice was so deep it bounced against her chest.

"None?" Thinking of Andrew and Father, she couldn't imagine the loneliness of no family. "I'm sorry," she murmured.

He didn't answer. Instead, he took her plate, set the dirty dishes in the pan she had used for mush, and filled it with water.

"I'll do that," she offered and hunched down on her knees. Swaying slightly, she stiffened her spine to steady herself. Using her hands as one, she scoured the dishes, shaking the water from them and letting the heat from the fire dry each item before she passed it to him. Silently, he took each dish and tucked it inside the saddlebags. She could feel his eyes watching her, measuring her. Was he questioning her change of attitude? Or, her throat tightened, was he assessing her qualities as a wife? A shudder rippled up her spine and blurred her vision. He had made no secret of what his intentions were.

The rope chafed her wrists as he stood. Her heart fluttered and she jumped up, rocking on the balls of her feet. Lights flashed before her eyes from the sudden movement. She bunched her hands into a fist. But he turned away and bent to untie a bedroll from the saddlebag.

"Here." He handed it to her then turned to get the other roll.

She stared at the bundle in her arms. Questions raced through her mind. When? Where? How would he force himself on her? She clenched her teeth until her jaws ached and answered the question herself. Never. She would find a way to stop him. But he was so strong. How could she protect herself?

Another verse she'd learned slipped into her mind.

He will not suffer thy foot to be moved: he that keepeth thee will not slumber.

It was a verse from one of Father's favorite psalms. She clung to the comfort of the words and thoughts of her father's love.

Brewster was spreading the blankets on the ground next to the saddle, the rope between them hindering his movements.

Staring at his back, she tried to still the panic shaking her knees. The rope between them meant she had to place her own blankets less than five feet away. She shuddered. Everything in her cried for space.

Tugging the other saddle as far from him as the rope would allow she let the bundle drop in a heap. Gritting her teeth, she settled herself on the blankets, sitting stiff and upright against the saddle.

Turning away, he pulled the slicker around his shoulders. He could have been made of stone for all the movement she saw after that. Stubbornly, she kept her face toward the fire, determined to ignore him, yet sharply aware of him. He was so close she could have reached out and touched him. Every nerve in her body was taut with apprehension.

"You might as well get comfortable." At the sound of his deep-voiced rumble, her nerves twitched. "We got a long ride tomorrow."

Crossing her arms across her chest, she squirmed down until her head rested against the saddle. Let him think she was settling down to sleep. She'd lie quiet and relaxed until he fell asleep, then. . .

Her head toppled toward her chest, jerking her to dull awareness. The fire had burned down to twisting, glowing embers. She held herself still for several thudding heartbeats, watching Brewster's back for any sign of wakefulness. His shoulder rose and fell with soft regularity. Filling her lungs slowly, Abby eased the blanket down to her ankles and drew her legs close to her body, tensing her muscles. Inch by cautious inch, she pulled the slack rope toward her until it hung between them in a gentle curve. It poured from Abby's hand, bridged the space between them, and crossed his body. Although she couldn't see it, she knew it was wrapped around his fist. She watched it sway hypnotically with the motion of his breathing and held her breath, waiting, her heart pounding in her ears. Slowly, silently, she eased air into her lungs. With trembling fingers, she inched the rope into her palm until it grew taut. Tugging very gently she tried to free it from his grasp, but it grated against the slicker. Stifling her disappointment, she let the rope relax, gathered her feet under her, and pushed herself up like a silent puff of smoke. Leaning toward him, she lifted the rope until it swayed above his body. Again, she raveled it in until it was taut, and gently tugged. The rope came alive in her hands, jerking her off balance. Reaching out to steady herself, her bound hands clawed at his shoulder. The fabric of his slicker, stiff and rough, rasped at her skin and she could feel his warmth beneath her palms. Gasping, she teetered on her feet, scrambling to keep from falling on top of him.

"You'll never get away." His voice rumbled beneath her fingertips and she fell back to her heels. Turning, he flipped the rope and it snaked between them like a living thing. "Now settle down."

She turned and met his eyes. His hat had fallen off and lay between them. For the first time, she saw his face without protection but it was too dark for her to make out anything but a shadowy outline.

He leaned forward and hissed, "I don't sleep much." There was no mistaking the tone of his voice. "Besides." He held out his open hand and she saw that the rope remained secure. He had tied it to himself.

Her chest collapsed as hope died and she shuffled back to the blanket, edging as far away as possible before she flipped on her side to stare into the darkness. Her pulse was still beating erratically and she concentrated on calming her breathing. He made no move to touch her but she fancied she could feel his hot breath against the back of her neck. She could sense his eyes boring into her and she suppressed an urge to whimper. To bring her breathing back to normal she filled her lungs and exhaled quietly in a slow, steady rhythm. She had to calm herself so she could think. Running had proved a disaster. Trying to gain his confidence and make him careless seemed futile. The permanent scowl sculpting deep creases in his face reminded her that he seldom let down his guard. There seemed little she could do while it was still dark and he had her shackled to him. Perhaps tomorrow would bring more opportunities. Surely, he would release her for a little privacy. She remembered what he had said about riding a long distance. The second horse gave her hope she would have her own mount. She would stay alert and grab whatever chance she could find.

The darkness swirled and throbbed around her, but she could not relax. When she closed her eyes, a dark-cloaked figure loomed above her, intimidating and silent. The rope chafed at her wrists and her neck hurt from using the saddle as a headrest. She was tired and knew the next day would be even more exhausting than this one had been, but she was afraid to fall asleep. As long as she stayed awake, she could see and hear his every move. If she slept, she was easy prey. She prayed for morning to come. She prayed for someone to rescue her. She prayed for mercy.

A sharp rock jabbed into her hip and she shifted to find a smoother spot on the cold, unforgiving ground. An owl hooted, its low mournful voice sending a shudder through her body. There was a quick rustling in the underbrush and she peered around the clearing for four-legged intruders. The tall pines were black giants moaning high overhead. The saddle under her cheek smelled of old leather and horse sweat. It wasn't an unpleasant smell, because it reminded her of her father. Often he'd come home with the smell of leather and warm horseflesh clinging to his clothes. After supper, it was his habit to sit in the rocker and read. She could picture him now with a book in his lap. Whenever she needed comfort or just his company, she would drop to the floor at his knees. He would put his finger in the book and lift it off his knee to make way for her to press her head to his lap. Father would pat her head as he rocked. Even now, she could feel the rocking motion and hear the chair's creak. Funny she should think of Father and the comfort of his rocking chair now. It would have made more sense to think of Andrew astride his horse riding in pursuit of them.

But maybe not so strange after all. Father's quiet presence had been her mainstay during her growing up years. He didn't say much, but he was there. And it was at his knee that much of her training had taken place. It was there she had learned to trust God's goodness and love. Never had she needed that confidence more than she did right now.

She drifted awake as the smell of coffee tickled her nose. Instinctively, she reached out to push herself upright and cried out, falling back as pain shot through her wrists. Her arms were cramped from their unnatural confinement and her wrists were on fire. Suddenly, she noticed the rope was slack and the end lay on the ground. Struggling to a sitting position, she awkwardly pushed her hair out of her face. She stared at the end of the rope, possibilities churning through her mind.

"Don't try it."

Flopping back on the blankets, she stared up into the narrow patch of blue. She should have played possum until he moved away. But it was too late now. Sighing loudly, she sat up again and watched him stirring something in the pot. Probably cornmeal again, but what difference did it make? As long as it kept up her strength so she could get away when the time came. And she was certain the opportunity would come.

Feeling like she had been tumbled over a pile of rocks, she pushed herself to her feet. Bending stiffly, she picked up the end of the rope, and with as much dignity as her creaking bones would allow, marched toward the forest, silently daring him to question her.

"Remember, I can track a mouse—"

"I know," she muttered. "Up a tree in a rainstorm."

"Yup. Don't be long."

Gritting her teeth to keep from retorting, Abby pushed her way into the trees until, glancing over her shoulder, she could no longer see him. She leaned against the rough bark of a pine tree, letting the tension drain from her body. The branches caught at her hair. How would she ever get the needles from her curls? She didn't even have a comb with her. Her wrists burned. A tear dribbled down her nose and she wiped it away. She knew the sun was shining overhead, by the bits of brightness flashing through the upper branches, but they did nothing to relieve the gloom on the forest floor. Slowly turning full circle, she studied her surroundings. There was nothing around her but trees and tangled undergrowth. She already knew the futility of trying to make her way through it. Futile or not, she had to get away. Muffling a sob, she bent her head and bit at the rope. Curling back her lips, she used her molars to grasp the coils. The rope burned at the corner of her mouth and her teeth ached. The rope grew wet with saliva, but she failed to loosen it.

"Arrgh." Her voice grew urgent as she continued to strain.

"Time's up." His call thudded into her frenzy.

If her brain weren't laced with spears of panic, she might almost imagine it was a game like one she had played often with Andrew when they were children. *Come out, come out, wherever you are.* Only this wasn't a game. Abby had no doubt her life was winding away and a deep shudder settled in the pit of her stomach.

Wiping her mouth, she flung her way back through the heavy growth, praying that Brewster's mind would be on continuing the journey and not on making good on his threat to take her as his wife. Hah! What a laugh! A wife was loved and cherished—not kidnapped and terrorized. What he planned to do to her had nothing to do with love and marriage, or a husband-wife relationship. He could call it whatever he wanted but it was pure and simple torture. Hesitating as she broke into the clearing, she stared at his back as he hunched over the fire, letting all her anger and fear blaze through her eyes as they bored into his black-shrouded figure. Too bad looks couldn't kill or he would fall face first into the fire.

"Food's ready." His words made her swallow hard, and blink. Handing her a bowl of mush, his eyes lingered on the rope at her wrist where the wetness was plain to see. She met his look squarely. He said nothing, nor did he take the end of the rope in his fist. It was as if he knew she could try whatever she wanted with no chance of success. Her jaw tightened against already sore teeth. If her bound hands hadn't made it difficult she would have thrown the mush in his face. Instead, she turned her back to him and stomped across the clearing. She bent her head. No words of thanks came to mind as she stared at the food. Then, realizing she would need to keep up her strength for the moment when God would provide a way of escape, she silently thanked Him for the provisions and ate in silence, biting down a cry of pain as she struggled to bring the spoon to her mouth. She let her resentment burn into a roaring fire as rawness stung her wrists. His footsteps thudded across the ground. From beneath his eyelashes, she saw him roll up the bedrolls and tie them to the saddles. Without lifting her head or turning around, she knew when he brought the horses to stand by the almost dead fire and heard him exhale as he tossed first one saddle, then the other onto their backs.

"Time to go." She hadn't heard him move toward her and the sound of his voice just a few inches away made her hands twitch. Why did he have to sneak around like that? She refused to look up. She wasn't going to move from this spot. Let him try to make her.

In a flash she recalled how he had thrown her into the saddle the day before, and she jumped to obey. Turning her head to avoid him, she marched to the side of the smaller horse. She stared at the stirrup and lifted her gaze to the saddle. She couldn't do it with her hands tied. Unless. . .she swung her wrists over the saddle horn, biting her lip against the pain. The horse sidestepped and Abby shuffled after it. She could taste blood but kept her teeth clamped firmly. Lifting her foot, she tried to wiggle it into the stirrup but her skirt caught her leg and she struggled to regain her balance, sweat beading on her brow. Before she could try again, he grasped her waist and lifted her. She swung her leg over the saddle and allowed him to settle her.

All the anger and frustration she had bottled up since she awoke, erupted in a burst of words. "If you would untie me, I could take care of myself." She glared down at him, feeling her eyes sting with resentment.

Pushing his hat back so he could see, he looked up at her, eyes dark and measuring. She waited, and when he didn't move away, she held her hands toward him. She could feel her heart beating in her chest as she waited. Finally, he dug in the pocket of his denim trousers and pulled out a knife. With practiced ease, he thumbed out a blade. Grabbing her fists, he sawed through the ropes.

She couldn't breathe. His grasp was gentle as he held her hands in his palm. He had enough power in his hands to crush her. She felt dizzy. He cut through the last coil and tossed the frayed scraps into the ashes before folding the knife and shoving it back into his pocket.

"Thank you," she whispered, rubbing her reddened skin. She was grateful that his attention was on coiling up the length of rope so he couldn't see her confusion. She almost wished he had left her bound. It was easier to deal with a man who was cruel and cared little for her comfort.

He tied the loops to his saddle, then swung up. Reaching back, he took the halter of Abby's horse.

"Let's ride," he rumbled.

three

They rode through the trees into a pocket clearing.

"This here's as good as any." His low nonchalant growl did not deceive her. She knew he'd picked this place with care, perhaps days ago. Throughout the long, hot hours of the day she had followed in his wake, climbing hills, skirting rocks, and wading noisy mountain streams. Abby's eyes were sharp enough to recognize the same narrow stream they crossed three times during the afternoon. She understood he was laying a carefully convoluted trail that would confuse the most expert tracker. For the last three hours they had climbed gradually until they were high into the rocky slopes of the mountains. He was meticulous in the execution of his plan.

She couldn't recall ever feeling such mind-numbing fatigue. They had stopped hours ago for a bit of dry biscuit and warm water. Since then, he had offered her his canteen several times. She had refused until she was almost choking on a combination of dust and fear. She almost gagged now as she thought of how thorough were his preparations. How could she hope to escape? Blinking back tears, she wondered what she had done to deserve such a fate. It hardly seemed fair that he'd noticed her in the short time they had been in the country.

It took her a moment to realize he had pulled his horse to a halt under the trees and had slid down, and was now reaching for the bridle of her mount. Before she could think to protest, he came to her side and lifted her from the saddle.

Her legs wobbled with the shock of her weight. She grabbed blindly for something to steady herself and her fingers brushed against his hand as he reached out to grasp her elbow. Revulsion shivered up her spine and she twisted away, gritting her teeth as she forced herself to stand unaided.

"I'm not used to riding." She grated the words over clenched teeth, biting hard to keep her teeth from rattling.

Now he'll make good on his threat to make me his wife. Her skin crawled at the thought. She almost gagged again. Apart from the hugs and kisses she'd received from Andrew and her father she'd never been touched by a man. They had been there to protect her from any passing dalliance. Not that they had needed to. She had never felt the need for romance. Andrew and Father were all she needed. She fixed her eyes on the ground, aware that she was quivering visibly.

"You can help gather firewood," he said in his low, grating voice, and she hurried after him, welcoming the gift of another few minutes.

Swathed in the scent of pine needles, they scoured the forest floor. Soon she had her arms full of dry kindling. He turned toward her, the ever-present slicker swinging out behind him like a billowing tent, filling her nose with the smell of old canvas. She stared at the slicker, wondering how he could stand to wear it everywhere. Despite the heat of the afternoon he had not once removed it, merely opening it wide so the wind could blow up underneath. He had eaten in it, slept in it, and rode in it. She wondered if it ever came off his body.

Seeing her arms full, he shifted his own load closer and strode back to the clearing. She scurried after him.

Efficiently and quickly, he built a roaring fire, and while waiting for it to burn down to hot embers, he turned to face her.

This is it, she thought. *The moment I pay the price.* And as he moved toward her, a prickling sensation crept across her skin. Despite the evening coolness, sweat beaded on her forehead and dribbled between her breasts.

A shudder raced up her spine as he stood close enough that she could catch the scent of pine and wood from the forest and oil from his slicker. It was all she could do to remain motionless, arresting the screams that roiled in the back of her throat.

"Supper will be a minute but don't get any ideas. I could track you over a pile of rocks so don't even think of running," he warned. His words seemed to come from a hollow deep within him. He glowered down at her from under the shade of his hat and then turned away, crossing to the horses to check their tethers.

Shuffling toward the fire, she held her hands toward the flames, as dizziness stole her strength. The heat could do nothing to warm the cold fear in the depths of her heart.

Behind her she heard the rattle of tin dishes. She flinched as he suddenly crouched next to her, fashioned a tripod over the glowing fire, and secured an iron pot full of beans. Within moments, the deep, rich smell bubbled up and she realized how hungry she was. Perhaps eating was of primary concern to Brewster at this moment too, because he showed no interest in her. Some of the tension seeped away, making room for her to become aware of other sensations.

"I need to go into the bushes," she murmured.

He nodded. "Go then."

Gathering her skirts, she held her head high and walked into the forest.

She felt relief at being alone and for a few minutes, she reveled in her freedom, acutely aware of the soft beauty of the evening. Beside her, a half dozen leather-colored butterflies clung to a decayed stump. The late afternoon sun poured golden light through the trees, and the air was filled with the sounds of a hundred birds busy in the treetops. Then a heavier sound, the muffled thud and crackling rustle of a larger animal silenced the birds and sent warning spears prickling across her skin.

For a heartbeat she hesitated before deciding she preferred a human attacker to the clutches of a wild animal. She turned and hurried back to the clearing, slowing her steps as she broke from the shelter of the trees. Praying that the racing of her heart and the flush of her flight did not show on her face, she stepped toward the fire.

Brewster watched impassively.

What did he see? she wondered. Could he see the fear in her eyes? Did he see her relief at seeing him lounging against his saddle? She turned her face downward, hoping that if he had noticed her reactions he wouldn't misinterpret them.

"Coffee's ready," he murmured, picking up a cup and pushing himself to his feet. He jerked to a stop. Abby followed his gaze and saw two men creep from the shadows, guns pointing straight at Brewster's chest.

"Don't do nothin' stupid," said one of the men. Behind him, the second man cackled.

Abby's scalp crawled. The flow of saliva that filled her mouth at the smell of coffee and beans drained instantly, leaving her tongue furry and stiff.

This is how the end feels, she thought, wondering at how calm she felt. Whoever these men were and whatever they wanted, she knew she wouldn't live to remember it.

From the corner of her eye, she saw Brewster facing the men, his hands still holding the cup in front of him. The flesh around his eyes was taut. She could almost feel his dark eyes glowering at the men. His rifle was propped like a lazy sentinel against his saddle, just out of reach and unavailable against the rifle and handgun held by the others.

Abby quickly turned her attention back to the two men.

"Get the gun," ordered the bigger of the two, and his sidekick scurried to obey. In the half light, Abby saw his face was pinched and narrow behind grimy whiskers. A sour, acidic smell stung her nostrils—a smell as evil as anything she'd imagined. The skin on the back of her neck crawled.

As slowly as she could manage, she began to back away.

"Hold it." The bigger man spun the gun in her direction and she stopped. "You watch him, Petey," he ordered the smaller man, nodding toward Brewster, and he took a step toward Abby.

"Well, well. Lookee here," he jeered. "A little chicken ripe for plucking."

"Hee, hee. And yer jest the one to do it. Right, Sam?"

"Durn tootin', I am." He leered, his narrow eyes gleaming, brown tobacco juice drooling out the corners of his mouth.

Every muscle in her body tightened as she measured the distance to the woods.

Understanding her intention, he lunged at her. With a muffled scream, she twisted away but he caught her arm, crushing it in a cruel grip. "It'd be a shame to let good game like this get away, wouldn't it, Petey?"

Petey cackled his agreement. "Do it, Sam. You first, then me."

"No," she moaned, the sound coming from the pit of her stomach. *I'll die first,* she vowed. She turned her eyes toward Brewster in a silent appeal for help and then Sam's rough hand grasped her and dragged her toward him. He wrapped both arms around her, pinning her to his chest. She exploded in his arms, kicking and thrashing violently, twisting her head wildly until she was forced to stop and catch her breath.

He laughed, his breath rancid against her face. "We got us a real fighter. Some get really feisty in rutting season."

Bursts of red flashed inside her head. His breathing was rapid, and she realized he was excited by her efforts to escape.

With a deep-throated groan, she sank her teeth into the fleshy part of his shoulder and bit so hard she could feel the flesh crunch. She gagged at the overwhelming stench, but hung on.

He roared and grabbed her hair, jerking her backwards, sending shafts of light ripping through her brain. She yanked her arm free and slapped him, only distantly aware of the sting in her palm.

With an angry grunt, he trapped her fist and in one quick movement, twisted her arm behind her back, pushing it upward until she cried out in pain. He laughed.

"Now that's better, ain't it?" He released his grasp on her hair and trailed his dirty hand down her throat and chest. His skin was rough, scraping her flesh like sandpaper. As he moved to do it again, she spat in his face.

"You ugly, bucktoothed son of Satan," she growled and spat again.

With an angry curse, he slapped the side of her head. Her vision disappeared into flashing, dancing lights and a roaring filled the air.

Sam released her abruptly, and she staggered, shaking her head in an attempt to clear it. Blinking her eyes to see past the pinprick lights filling her vision, she saw Brewster facing the pair, his legs spread wide, knees slightly bent, arms raised to reveal clenched fists. He roared like an angry bear. Petey staggered backward as Brewster exploded into his face. With a thrust that sent Petey reeling, Brewster leapt across the clearing, closing the distance between himself and Sam, who spun on his heel at the sound of a wild animal charging.

"Why, you ugly monster," he snarled and raising his gun, slammed it into the side of Brewster's head. Brewster staggered, knees buckling, but he did not go down.

"Run, Abigail," he growled. "Take my horse." With an upward jerk, he drove both fists into Sam's chin, spinning him backward.

Abby didn't hesitate. She dashed toward the horses, thinking perhaps none of the men would survive. And she didn't care. A burning emotion flooded her brain. *Where on earth had such animals come from?*

With Brewster's roars thundering in her ears, she darted across the clearing. Brewster's bigger horse was closest. Grabbing the halter, she swung him around. Clutching handfuls of rough mane, she vaulted herself into the saddle. Behind her, the sound of grunts and thuds shuddered up her spine. She hesitated. Should she kick the horse into the forest or try to race across the clearing to the narrow pathway they had followed earlier in the evening? Her heart catching in her throat, she reached down and gathered the halter of the second horse, clucking them both into motion. Ducking under the branches, she paused at the edge of the clearing.

Sam lay face down, perilously close to the glowing embers. A motionless Petey stared up at the darkening sky, blood streaming from his mouth and nose. She saw them both in a flash and turned to locate Brewster. He rocked back and forth on his hands and knees, his head hanging almost to the ground. Blood dripped from his nose. Before she could change her mind, she guided the horses forward.

"Get on," she choked out.

Brewster raised his head and looked vacantly at her.

She stared down at him. As he huddled on the ground he looked harmless. Her brain screamed for her to race away, but she couldn't move. Her heart echoed inside her chest, which seemed suddenly hollow. Brewster had risked his life to save her from Petey and Sam—she felt she owed him something for that. But wait! He had placed her in harm's way in the first place.

The urgency to escape warred with the fledgling reluctance to abandon him to his bloody fate. Suddenly—with blinding clarity—she remembered that she was lost in the woods without him.

She slid from the horse and pulled it toward him, reaching one hand out to grab his arm. "Get up," she begged. "Come on, we've got to get out of here." Behind her one of the men moaned. "Hurry."

Brewster staggered to his feet, weaving unsteadily, and gave his head an unsteady shake. His eyes rolled back and she grabbed him as he tipped to the side.

"Brewster. Stay with me." She pushed him toward the horse. He leaned his forehead into its flank and a long shudder raced through his body.

"Get on," she urged, panic making her voice thin.

"Wait," he mumbled. "Guns. Food."

"Never mind that." A grunt behind her made her sure the men would be on them again. "We have to hurry."

"Get them."

Recognizing the stubbornness in his growl, she grunted

with exasperation and turned to look for the items. The saddlebags lay close to the fire, and she gingerly picked them up, avoiding looking at the inert men. When Petey groaned, she jumped back.

"The rifle too," he whispered, taking a pistol from the saddlebags and jamming it into his waistband. Wasting no time arguing, she ran toward the saddle and scooped it up. Spinning on her heel, she hurried back to the horses. Grabbing the saddlebags from his clutches, she flung them over the horses.

"Get on," she ordered, pushing on his back as he tried to lift himself to the animal's back. For a moment, she thought he was going to fall off the other side, but he moaned, shifted his weight and held on.

Hurrying, she pulled herself on the second horse and clucked the horses into action.

"I'll get you for this." The roar from Sam made Abby kick her horse in the ribs. He bolted down the trail. When they came out of the trees into a narrow strip of grass, she reined her horse in the direction from which they had come.

"Left," Brewster mumbled. "Go left."

Before she could argue, he took the lead, guiding his mount along a trail that rose briskly into the mountains. Her mouth was dry with panic, but she followed closely on the heels of his horse.

They managed to keep up a steady pace, though Brewster swayed, riding with his head bobbing on his chest. He seemed to know instinctively where they were, several times indicating they should veer slightly in a different direction. They entered a rock-strewn hilly area, their progress slowed as they climbed, picking their way over and around rocks often as big as a house. She continually wondered how Brewster could tell where he was going in the moonless night. A few minutes before, he had reached over and taken the lead rope of her horse. Somehow, he seemed to be able to find the invisible path, which couldn't have been any wider than the horses' hooves.

Suddenly he lurched to a stop and the horses waited in single file, the sound of their breathing loud and rough in the still night.

"Get down," Brewster ordered, his words gruffer than usual. She knew he was struggling to remain conscious and she prayed he wouldn't pass out and leave her alone in the choppy sea of boulders and strange shapes.

Sliding from the back of her mount, she prayed there would be place to set her feet, and discovered a thin strip of gravel behind the horse. She grimaced as she heard Brewster grunt when he slid down. In the dimness, she could make out his shape. He swayed like a pendulum, then pushed himself upright and pulled his horse forward. She looked up as her horse followed. Before them were more rocks, seemingly a mountain of them rising right to the sky. Stumbling, she grabbed for support, scraping her palm on the rough boulder at her side. It was surprisingly warm. Suddenly, the ground leveled and she saw that the rocks gave way to a black wall. Brewster stepped into the blackness and disappeared, pulling the horses in after him.

"Come on," he rumbled.

She stepped forward into the black unknown. Brewster and the horses disappeared in the thick blackness. She stopped. In the darkness it was impossible to tell if a bottomless pit lay at her feet. With a mouth as dry as desert sand, she felt around with both hands. There was nothing. The air in her lungs rushed to her throat in a lump that almost choked her. She strained to hear a sound that would give her a clue to Brewster's whereabouts.

"Keep a comin'."

She never thought she would feel relief at hearing his rough voice, but had to hold back a cry. She stepped forward, hands out to guide her.

"We'll be safe in here. As long as they don't track us across the rocks." His voice was immediately to her right and she turned, bumping into the broad warm flank of a horse. A hand came out and grabbed her arm.

"Right here's the wall. Just sit down and keep quiet."

She put her hands against the rough damp walls and lowered her weary body to the ground, refusing to think about what might be underneath her. Beside her, Brewster shuffled about and grunted. His shape was barely discernible, but knowing he was there made her feel a smidgen safer. Slowly her toes uncurled and the tension inside her stomach loosened. The muscles in her legs began to uncramp. She was too exhausted to feel fear, even though in the back of her mind she knew that her situation had not improved. Not only was she in captivity to a man who made his plans for her very plain, now there were two men on their trail. Sam did not look like the kind of man who would be happy until he had extracted his pound of flesh in payment for the humiliation Brewster had poured on him.

The clouds sailed away and the moon dribbled silver light on the rocks outside the cave. She could make out Brewster leaning against the wall, turned toward the opening, watching. He had lost his hat in the fight and in the wan light, he had a ghostly pallor. He swung to the right, carefully studying the scene, and she saw dark dribbles seeping down his neck.

He'd risked his life for her. Whether to protect his own interests or out of genuine concern for her safety, she didn't know. And it didn't matter. She owed him for what he had done.

Still, she couldn't stop a burst of satisfaction at the sight of his injury. He deserved no less for the misery he had inflicted on her with his crude way of seeking a wife.

A wave of guilt blurred her vision. She wouldn't have left an animal to suffer unattended. And he had been injured saving her.

The scene at the fire raced through her mind. Brewster leaping across the fire to attack Sam, ignoring the risks involved. What had triggered his foolhardy rescue? She shuddered as she remembered Sam's roughness and rubbed the side of her head where he had slapped her. Realization flooded her mind.

It had been when Sam slapped her that Brewster roared into action.

She dashed away hot tears and stared at Brewster. A surge of gratitude warmed her. He didn't have to risk his life for her. He could have waited until Sam and Petey were doing what they planned and escaped without their notice. For a moment, her fear of him and her anger at what he had done vanished. She wanted to convey her appreciation.

She shuffled toward him, kneeling close to his side. "You're injured," she murmured, reaching out to touch the wound on his temple.

Her fingers barely touched his brow before he jerked away, turning to face her. His scowl darkened his features. "Leave it be."

"But it should be cleaned," she murmured, thinking she had startled him from his concentration on the scene outside the mouth of the cave. "There's blood all through your hair." *Perhaps,* she thought, *his wound is causing him pain.* "I'll be careful."

"Don't bother." He turned away, his words as cold as steel.

His refusal stung her. "I was only trying to help."

"It'll heal without your help."

His tight words were so full of icy dismissal she felt as if he had hollered at her to get lost. He shook off her offer of help like it was a bad smell. Her eyes burned. This man was as unlikable as any she'd met. He couldn't go around refusing to accept people's kindly offers without offending someone. No wonder he wore a permanent scowl. Her resentment could not be stemmed. "I suppose that's what happened to your face," she lashed out at him. "You got cut in a fight and refused to take care of it."

She sat back on her heels, breathing hard.

Inch by inch, as if turning on a rusty hinge, he pivoted toward her. A lump of dread settled in the back of her throat. She knew she shouldn't have spoken those words. She would have taken them back if it were possible but now all she could do was wait for the unleashing of his anger.

His eyes were dark and unreadable in the dim light and yet she felt them boring into her, impaling her with their intensity. He seemed so tense—tightly coiled like a man who is holding himself in, or, she thought in a flash of understanding, like a man holding himself above things.

"You're right on, except for a few details," his voice was heavy with sarcasm. "I was five years old and it was my mother who did this."

four

The silence between them was thick in the dank closeness of the cave. Somewhere behind her she heard a faint rustle. A shiver raced across her neck. She stared at him, certain she had misunderstood the venom in his voice.

"Your mother?" she gasped. "You mean you were hurt in an accident."

Brewster continued to look straight ahead, his eyes dark and empty. She knew he stared right through her.

"It was no accident." His voice was low and flat, but the sound of the pain he tried to disguise tore through her.

"Oh, Brewster." There was so much she longed to say. To ask. Surely, it was a misunderstanding. No mother would purposely injure a child. Especially her own.

Even the black slicker did not hide the hunch of his shoulders or the rigid way he held his neck. "Forget it."

His voice was so deep it thundered through Abby. She shuddered and pressed her lips together to keep from crying out.

"But. . ." She longed to say she was sorry, but the words stuck in her throat, choked back by her confusion. How could she feel pity for this man?

"Forget it, I said." The brittleness in his voice killed any sympathy that had bubbled unbidden to the surface. She blinked back angry tears.

Fresh blood, black in the dim light, oozed past his right eye. It spread along his cheek over the tracks of the already-dried patches.

Cuts and blood were not unfamiliar to her. She had doctored many wounds for Andrew and Father. Father always said she was a good little nurse, teasing her because she was so particular about keeping even small cuts clean and covered. Swallowing back her revulsion at the thought of touching him, she tried again.

"Please, let me clean your wound." She tried to keep her voice from shaking, hoping she sounded pleasant, maybe even cheerful.

He stared out at the moonlit rocks, as impassive as a drugstore Indian.

A shudder raced down her spine. If his injuries were worse than she thought, she could never hope to find her way out of these rocks. And if Sam and Petey were to find them—

She trembled, remembering the stench of Sam's nearness. Nausea welled up and she forced herself to breathe deeply.

Slowly, as if the movement took all his effort, he nodded. She wondered whether he was agreeing. He leaned forward to rest his arms on his knees.

Not giving herself a chance to change her mind, she bent and ripped a strip from her petticoat. The canteen lay beside him and she poured a little water on her rag then edging closer, leaned toward him. Her nostrils flared with the oily smell of his slicker and the metallic scent of blood. And something more. She could smell his warm flesh—pine scent mixed with the salty smell of sweat. For an instant, she wondered what strange mixture composed this man. Then, narrowing her eyes and filling her lungs with the stagnant air that seeped down from the ceiling of the cave, she pressed the wadded cloth to his forehead.

"I'll have to probe around this wound a bit. I'll be as careful as I can." Her nerves were as ragged as the bit of cloth she had torn from her petticoat. In order to keep her fingers steady, she resorted to her usual way of calming herself. She talked as she worked. It was the way Andrew and she had always dealt with pain or problems. They talked to each other. Although there was no twin-bond with this man, she needed the comfort of words.

"I've taken care of injuries before," she murmured. "Andrew

seemed to always be getting himself scraped up, falling out of trees, or gouging his knees on the gravel, or jamming his hand into something sharp."

Beneath her fingers the blood was warm and sticky.

"There's gravel in here," she muttered. "You must have rolled in the dirt after you were hit."

He grunted a reply, and as she picked the bits out, she felt him trembling.

"I'm sorry. I'm being as careful as I can."

"It don't bother me."

As near as she could determine in the dim light, the wound was about three inches long. From the width of the gash, she guessed it was fairly deep, but there was little that could be done, other than to clean it as much as possible with the limited water supply and try to stop the bleeding. She knew it must be painful. Yet, apart from the slight trembling, he gave no indication—not even a grunt—as she pressed her fingers against the wound, plucking out the bits of bark and rock.

"I wish I had a light," she grumbled, more to herself than for his benefit. "It's impossible to see how clean this is."

"It don't matter much," he rumbled.

"But it does," she insisted. "If I can get it clean it lessens the chance of infection. Now hang on, I'm going to apply some pressure." She turned the soiled rag over and folded it to a clean side then pressed it to the cut.

Again, she felt him quiver and she touched his shoulder in sympathy. "I know it hurts but I have to stop the bleeding."

"It doesn't hurt. I never hurt."

It had to hurt like mischief. She glanced down at his fists clenched around his knees. Even in the pale light she could see the knuckles white and gleaming.

She shook her head. Tense as a cat about to spring, yet silent and stoic about his pain—her sense of who this man was grew more and more confused. Lifting her compress, she leaned close. She heard his breath scraping over his teeth. She guessed that he held himself with a very taut rein and she wondered at the tension in him.

The bleeding had slowed, but not stopped entirely, so she continued to apply pressure. For a moment, she studied his profile, pale in the flat light. His expression was hard, as if etched eons ago in the granite walls of the cave.

Cautiously, she again lifted the cloth and was relieved to see that the bleeding had stopped. Now she could attend to cleaning up the rest of the blood.

"There isn't much I can do about the gunk in your hair until we get more water. I'll just sponge at it a little and do the best I can." His hair was heavy and coarse, matted with dirt and clots of blood.

She dampened the sticky spots with the soiled rag and eased out the worst of the dirt.

"I'll get rid of this mess on your neck." The blood had dried to stubborn crusts and she had to scrub at the area, resting her hand against his neck to steady herself. His skin was damp and cool. Like the air. Suddenly she realized how cold it was. No wonder he was shivering. The cave had the closed-in coldness of never being warmed by sunshine. Her fingers grew more brisk, scrubbing until the worst was gone.

She was filled with curiosity about this man. His voice was as expressionless as a piece of glass. He claimed he felt no pain. But how could he be as cold and unfeeling as he seemed, yet want companionship so badly that he turned to desperate means in order to acquire it? Part of her despised everything he stood for—the selfish hardness of him. But he had risked his life to save her. As if controlled by someone other than herself, she let her fingers slide down his damp neck. It felt strong and surprisingly smooth. A tingling raced up her fingertips and she shrank back, her cheeks burning. Beneath her breastbone, she felt a quickening and her breath caught in her throat.

"I'm done." Her words sounded breathless and strained. She plunked down beside him, careful to avoid touching him, and pressed her hands into her lap, trying unsuccessfully to stop the shivers coursing through her body.

She hated this man. It was his fault she wasn't safe at home with Andrew.

Andrew, she silently cried. She hadn't felt so cut off from him since childhood. There had been a time when she cried bitterly if she couldn't be with him. Father used to laugh and say they were like two halves of a ball. Without the matching half, they were nothing. He said it teasingly and lovingly, but she suspected there was a great deal of truth in it. She no longer cried when she and Andrew had to be apart, but with every passing hour, she felt farther and farther from him. She anguished over how he would feel. Would she ever see him again? A dagger pierced her gut and ripped toward her heart. She leaned forward and grasped her knees, stifling a moan.

Brewster turned toward her. "You hurt?"

"No," she mumbled, even as her pain and fear turned to burning hatred of this man. She eased her breath over her teeth and reminded herself that she needed him to get her out of this place.

Besides, she reminded herself, *God loves him.*

It was a strange thought and she wondered that God's love included both of them despite their vast differences. How could He love such a person? She shuddered as she reflected on the evilness of his plan.

"You're cold," Brewster muttered. "Here." He shrugged out of his voluminous slicker and thrust it around her shoulders.

"No, no." She shook her head, even as she welcomed its warmth. "You keep it." She didn't want to feel any more in his debt. It was hard to be angry at a man who saved your life and then made sure you were warm while he sat stoically ignoring the cold. And she needed to be mad at him. She needed that defense. Something about him called to a place in her heart where she sensed something deep and hungry—she didn't know what. She was afraid to look any deeper.

The smell of the warm canvas stirred a response from some hidden place, but she shrugged her shoulders and shook her head to chase any thoughts away. The slicker fell to the ground.

"You keep it," she insisted. "I'll be all right."

"Don't be crazy," he growled just a breath away from her ear. "The rest of our stuff is back at the campfire. You'll freeze without some protection." He picked the coat up from the floor and once again draped it around her shoulders.

"You'll get just as cold," she argued, still not willing to accept it.

"I don't feel the cold much," he said and turned back to his study of the landscape.

His attention was focused on something in the distance. He seemed to have forgotten her. She waited for a heartbeat before admitting defeat, then let her shoulders relax and pulled the veil of warmth about her, sniffing a bit at the canvas smell, and then breathing deeply as she searched her senses for the more elusive smells—the scent of old forests and strong dreams. She snorted softly at her thoughts. Determined once again to ignore them, she lifted her head, concentrating on the rocky scene below.

Abby noticed that Brewster was suddenly peering intently toward the horizon and a pang of alarm raced through her. She followed the direction of his gaze. In the distance, far to the right, there was a flare of orange.

"Is it a campfire?" she asked, almost certain of the answer without asking.

"Yup."

Despite his calm answer, she could sense his intense study of it. He tightened without moving like a man who comes upon a coiled rattlesnake.

She half rose. "Maybe it's Andrew. I know he's looking for me."

Brewster settled back again. "This brother of yours. . ."

"Twin," she interrupted.

He continued as if she hadn't spoken. "He done much tracking?"

"No. Why?"

"Then it ain't him. It'd take an Indian to follow the trail I left."

"Then—" Alarm skittered up and down her spine. "Indians?"

"We're pretty far from any Indians I know of."

"Sam and Petey?" A blend of disgust and fear made her voice crackle, and she tried to blink away the memory of Sam's face. His evil gleam seemed branded on her brain, along with the stench, and the way tobacco juice dribbled down his whiskers. Petey's lewd "hee-hee-hee" rang in her ears.

"Yup. That's my guess."

"Will they be able to follow us?"

"Can't say. Didn't take either of them for trackers."

What would have indicated they were? she wondered. But she supposed she knew what he meant. Somehow they didn't fit the picture of keen-eyed, sharp-witted trackers.

He continued staring at the flickering orange spot that was no bigger than a firefly.

"They're too close." Brewster's low, rough voice broke the tense silence. "We'll have to move before light." He hunkered down closer to his knees. "Best get some rest."

She stiffened at his suggestion. As if she could just order up sleep when she was trapped in a living, breathing nightmare. But the night was cool, and her mind refused to face any more problems. She lay down on the hard, cold ground and curled up on her side, pulling the warmth of the heavy coat around her.

Suddenly, she bolted upright and stared out at the darkness.

"What's the matter?" Brewster's low voice came from the darkness.

"Andrew," she gasped, too affected by her worry to care what this man might think. "What if he meets up with those two down there?"

"Your brother—your twin," he amended. "Is he a careful man?"

"What do you mean?"

"Would he chase after you without consideration? Would

he race down the trail, or watch for signs?"

She had to think about it. Andrew was so much a part of her she couldn't picture how he would act alone. And up until a few weeks ago, their lives had been simple and predictable. She had taken care of Andrew and Father. Andrew had worked at the mill. Suddenly, she recalled how he had always checked the belts and gears, and warned her to stay back when she had visited him. "Yes, he's careful."

"Then he wouldn't likely ride up to them unawares. They aren't exactly invisible."

His words soothed her fears and she lay down again, squirming around on the hard ground until she found a place halfway comfortable.

Andrew, she silently called, *be careful. God, be with him. Be with me. Get us all out of this mess.*

"Wake up." A hand jostled her shoulder.

"Go away, Andrew," she mumbled, shrugging away.

"Wake up."

The hand grew more insistent.

The voice! It wasn't Andrew's. She recoiled as all the details of the past two days filled her mind in a deluge of fear and terror and she retreated back into the warmth, wanting nothing more but to sink into oblivion until this nightmare ended.

"It's time to leave."

His deep rumble was firm, but she still huddled in a ball, reluctant to leave the shelter of sleep.

"You planning to be a welcoming party for our two friends down there? If you are, you'll be a party of one. I'm leaving." His boots thudded on the floor of the cave.

Ignoring the chill of the air, she sprang to her feet, clutching the slicker around her shoulders.

"Wait." Her voice broke. Her mouth was so dry she could hardly swallow and she wanted to call out for the canteen, but in the darkness she couldn't see where he was. Afraid he had already left, she stumbled toward the gaping area that was a shade lighter than the rest. "I'm coming." Suddenly, his figure loomed against the yawning opening. Her heart somersaulted with relief.

"I'm so thirsty."

"Have a drink, but go easy on it until we can refill."

She groped in the darkness for the canteen she knew he was holding toward her. She found his arm first. He remained motionless as she let her fingers scurry down the length of his limb until she found the canteen and removed it. Eagerly, she filled her mouth with water. It was stale but it was cool and wet. She kept the moisture in her mouth for several seconds before swallowing. Then she took three more large mouthfuls, screwed the lid on, and passed it back. In the darkness their hands met. In the blackness that surrounded her, contact with human flesh sent warm trickles up her arm.

She jerked her hand away and rubbed it on her skirt. It might be dark—and the darkness oppressive—and it might be spooky, but she detested this man and nothing would change that. Not even the shivers racing across her shoulders and the hand begging to reach out and know someone was out there.

"It's pitch-dark out." Her voice was sharper than she planned. "How can we go anywhere?"

"You'd rather wait 'til Petey and Sam are at the door?" His voice said how foolish he thought she was.

"No," she answered, stung by his sarcasm. "But neither do I want to fall down the side of a mountain."

"Best stick close then. I know the way." He clucked to the horses and they shuffled forward. "Come on."

Wondering if he meant her or the animals, she moved to obey and stumbled on the hem of the slicker. "Wait. I can't walk in this thing. What do you want me to do with it?"

His warm hand touched her head and slid down her neck. His fingers dug into her flesh as he lifted the coat from her shoulders. From the sounds beside her, she knew he had flopped it on the back of one of the horses. "You ready now?"

His every action was so sudden and decisive it left her groping for a response.

"Come on then."

His words thrust her into action and she stepped through the mouth of their shelter.

The forest-sweet air brushed her face and the stars winked overhead. She lowered her eyes to where they had seen the campfire but nothing relieved the blackness.

She followed him, sliding her feet past sharp rocks. She stifled a cry as her ankle raked against a razor-edged stone.

"Give me your hand," he whispered hoarsely. "I'll show you the way." He found her hand and gripped it tightly, his warmth a welcome contrast to the cold rocks. Inch by inch, he guided her along the path. She wanted to fling his hand away, yet she clung to his warm, hard hand, trusting him to direct her. The night was as black as the path beneath them. It was an eerie feeling, like walking across the sky.

He stopped. "We'll have to wait a bit. Just until there's light enough to see." He dropped her hand and she hugged it to her chest, glad to be free of contact yet fighting a spinning feeling of isolation.

The ground was still black but the stars had been rubbed out by a faint gray line across the horizon. They didn't have to wait long for the sky to lighten and as it did, the pathway slowly grew visible. Abby gasped. Ahead of them a sheer cliff rose from the gloom. At their feet, the mountain fell away into darkness.

"We're trapped." She half turned to see where they had come. "I thought you knew where we were going." Her voice was high with panic.

"Calm down," he muttered, his voice grating in the stillness. "There's a path across the face of the cliff."

"A path?" Her voice rose to a squeak. "You're joshing me." The cliff was sheer rock. Not a twig of branch or strip of dirt. Just straight up and straight down.

"You'll see. Just a few more minutes and it'll be light enough."

Light enough to die? she thought. If there had been any

doubt in her mind about his sanity, it had vanished. "You're crazy if you think I'm. . ."

"Hush. Sound carries for miles in this air."

She sputtered to silence as he raised his hand. He stood with his head tilted as if listening. She tipped her head to match his and strained to catch a sound.

There was nothing but the whisper of the pine branches. The sun edged over the horizon in a shout of orange and pink, filling the world with color, awakening the birds. And awakening the two men far below. Their voices carried to the cliff like echoes in the distance.

Abby's mouth was so dry her tongue stuck to the top of her mouth. She guessed if they made a sound, it would carry readily to the men below and she prayed they were too sleepy to look up. She shuddered at the her plight, trapped like an animal in a cage. Trapped by the mountain, Brewster, and the dirty men below.

"You'll have to go first," Brewster whispered. "I'll bring the horses."

She hesitated. She didn't want to leave the protection of the shadows. He nudged her gently and she shuffled toward the cliff, her fingers digging into the dirt at her back. Through squinted eyes, she saw the world drop off at her feet. Her head pounded like a hundred war drums.

"Don't look down," Brewster ordered. His whisper sounded like it came from the sighing treetops down the slope. "Look carefully to your right and you'll see a narrow ledge."

She followed his instructions. There was indeed a narrow ledge but she couldn't force herself to step into the blue-gray void. The world swirled and tipped. Brewster's hand caught her shoulder and squeezed.

"It's wider than it looks. I've crossed it and so have the horses."

"I can't." She leaned against the cliff, her eyes closed tightly.

"You can." His words were quiet and firm, but did nothing to relieve the quivering in her limbs. "Consider the alternatives."

She swallowed hard.

"You could go straight down. Not a pleasant thought. Or you could go back and wait for Sam and Petey."

"You mean I'm stuck between a rock and a hard place."

He snorted softly—a sound that could have been either mirth or derision. Given her choices, she turned toward the rock wall.

Brewster murmured instructions in her ear. "Take it slow and careful. Slide your feet one at a time." He kept up a slow, steady patter of words, which she clung to like a lifeline as she leaned into the cliff. Holding her breath, she willed her dizziness to stop and forced her eyes to focus on the ledge, telling herself it had to be wider than her fears reported. Hadn't Brewster said the horses had crossed it?

Her heart racing like a hard-run horse, she inched her foot sideways. Every muscle in her body tightened as she forced her leg to extend past her hip. Her chest rose and fell like a churning paddle, but she could not make herself shift her weight to the extended leg.

"Easy now." The words came from some place to her left, his grating voice jerking her free of her paralysis. "Just another inch and you'll be on the path."

She clenched her toes and leaned into her foot, feeling the coolness of the rocky ledge at her back.

"There you go. You've got it." His voice remained slow and calm, his words pushing her to take that first step, and then the next, and then another.

She kept her eyes focused on the barely visible cliff, clamping her jaw to keep her teeth from chattering.

Suddenly, a rock rolled from under her foot. She gasped as her foot slipped. She felt the color drain from her face and her stomach churned until she thought she would throw up. The rock skittered down the mountain, bouncing and banging, a sound like bells, announcing their whereabouts.

"Don't move."

He could have saved his breath. Frozen with fear, she couldn't have moved if she wanted.

"Yoo hoo." The sound was faint, like a distant whisper. Sam's voice was unmistakable as was Petey's accompanying, "Hee-hee-hee."

"Keep moving," Brewster whispered. "A few more feet and we'll be across this cliff. They'll never see us once we reach the trees."

Her muscles, stiff and unresponsive, felt like metal rods as she resumed her shuffling sideways gait. She caught a glimpse of swaying tree branches and slowly lifted her head. Safety and solid ground were just inches away. She threw herself toward the ground, clutching at a tree trunk as she gasped for air, letting the windstorm of fear subside into a sighing breeze. She turned to see what had become of Brewster. He was almost across the rock face, leading both horses.

He turned his head until he could see her. "You okay?" The bright morning sun caught the scar on his cheek. The irregularity of his features made him appear to be part of the rough bank behind him. She blinked to bring him into focus and called a soft, "Yes."

"Lookee, there they is."

Abby's eyes locked with Brewster's as Petey's faint chortle carried to them on the rising morning air.

"Looks like we got us a sitting duck. Too bad, you ugly monster." Sam's words echoed in the stillness.

Brewster's expression hardened. Abby didn't take time to consider his reactions. All she wanted was for him to get to safety.

"Hurry," she called, and he began to move again, but it was impossible to hurry on the narrow ledge.

A puff of dirt exploded beside Brewster's head, followed by a sharp crack.

She stared at him, not wanting to believe what she saw.

He was being shot at. She clamped her hand to her mouth.

Suddenly, Brewster recoiled like he'd been slapped and

grabbed his left shoulder. From below, she heard another crack of the rifle. Red seeped around Brewster's fingers as he clutched his arm.

He's been hit. She stared openmouthed at him then sprang forward, reaching a hand toward him.

"Brewster," she called, silently willing him to turn toward her. If he passed out and fell—

Her hand quivered. She didn't know how long it would take Sam and Petey to catch up to her and she didn't dare think about what would happen to her when they did.

"Give me your hand." She strained toward him but he shook his head. She could feel him take a deep breath and begin to move again. She prayed he would make it.

Another puff of dirt burst from the rocks, this time to Brewster's right. The far horse threw back its head, jerking Brewster's arm. Abby gasped, certain he was going to be thrown to his death. Brewster mumbled something to the horse and continued his snail-paced shuffle. Her pulse throbbed in her temples. Then he was close enough to raise his arm. His hand touched hers.

With fierce determination, she clamped her fingers around his, and wrapped her free arm around the trunk of a scraggly pine. He leapt the last foot, crashing into the branches of the closest tree, the horses nearly landing on top of him, and then she yanked him away from the treacherous edge. His weight carried her backward. With a lung-wrenching thud they landed in a heap on the soft forest floor.

She noted every detail with a sharp precision. His square jaw clenched so hard that the muscles in his face twitched. His scar slashed across his cheek. She had not seen his eyes so clearly before—deep, deep green pools, guarded and secretive. His whole expression was as bleak and hard as the rock cliff he had crossed.

Somewhere, deep in her being, something sparked and flared. Her lips parted as she fought to get air.

She took a long, shuddering breath as he lay beside her for

a moment then staggered to his feet and stood gasping. She noticed his sleeve was red with blood.

"You're bleeding."

He glanced at his arm with barely a flicker of interest. "It's nothing. Only a graze." And he turned his back on her, pulling the horses to him.

She sat up, a warm blush of anger racing up her cheeks. He didn't feel pain. He didn't feel cold. He never slept. He never felt anything. She was surprised he bled.

Let him bleed to death, or fall off a cliff. It would only make her life easier.

But what about Sam and Petey? And finding your way off this mountain? a little voice nagged.

She stood and smoothed her skirts though they were long past improvement.

Turning, she stared at Brewster's stiff back. She needed him. For now. But not for long.

He wiped his hands on his thighs, leaving dark streaks of blood down one pant leg. Without turning, he ordered her to follow him.

"From here, we climb," he announced over his shoulder.

five

Abby staggered along, forcing her reluctant legs to function.

They had spent the day climbing, backtracking, then climbing some more. At one point she looked up from her weary slouch to discover that they were back at the clearing where they had encountered Sam and Petey. She lifted her head and glanced around, afraid they'd ridden into a trap, but as Brewster dismounted and helped her down, there was no sign of Petey or Sam. She collapsed on a log and watched with weak interest as he recovered the saddles and the bag suspended from the tree that contained the bulk of their supplies. He pulled the horses into a thicket and tied them. Before she could fully catch her breath, they were once again on the move, following another nearly invisible trail.

Abby stumbled, but Brewster forged ahead, never looking back. She wondered if she were to collapse in a quivering heap behind him, would he come back for her? She doubted that he would, but she couldn't dredge up enough energy to feel anger or even hatred. Muscles she didn't know she owned screamed for rest.

Brewster's back loomed suddenly before her and she scuttled to a stop. Thinking they could rest, she sagged with relief and glanced around his shoulder. Above them loomed a shrub-laced hill. In the lengthening shadows she was certain there was no passage or pathway. Moaning weakly, she allowed weariness to wash through her. Her limbs quivered and she knew she lacked the strength to retrace her steps.

As she stood trembling, Brewster bent, parted some bushes, then pushed aside a rock. He stared into the shadowy depths, then grunted.

"Looks in good shape. In you go." Stepping aside, he

waved his arm for her to proceed.

She stared at him, her mouth working in confusion.

"Go ahead. There's a tunnel."

His face floated before her eyes. Too confused to argue, too weary to care where the tunnel led, she dropped to all fours, groaning at the dull ache in her back, and forced her arms to pull her into the blackness. The walls closed around her, damp and musty. The skin crawled on the back of her neck. How long must they be in this shaft, crawling along like animals? It was Brewster's fault. *I wouldn't be here if he hadn't had the notion to kidnap himself a wife.* But the anger she wanted to feel was merely a vague stirring in some distant corner of her heart. All she could think was, *Please, let's stop.* She leaned forward, letting her head almost touch the damp ground. She couldn't move another inch.

As if in answer to her silent plea, he spoke, his voice even deeper and more rasping than it had been in the open.

"There's an opening in front of you. It's a room. You can stand up."

She moved her hand forward slowly and felt empty space. She leapt back in alarm, banging into Brewster. "Sorry," she mumbled, red-hot embarrassment burning her cheeks. She let her hands feel down the walls of the dark room, found the bottom, then lowered herself headfirst out of the tunnel. The darkness was as deep as the inside of a well. It was impossible to fill her lungs.

"Move away so's I can get in."

His voice startled her and she gasped. Scuttling along on all fours, she stopped when she bumped into a cool wall.

She heard Brewster drop to the floor, then the scrape and thud of his boots on the earthen floor. A match flared, highlighting his features in a yellow puddle of light as he tipped the flame over a stubby candle. Flickering light wavered across the dark walls.

Abby glanced around. It was a very small room. Her gaze lingered on the narrow cot a few feet from where she crouched.

She lifted wide eyes toward Brewster. The sputtering candle-light threw dancing shadows across his face, distorting his features, giving him a hawklike appearance. She was beginning to understand that his piercing eyes and forbidding expression disguised a mind like a steel trap. The trail they had left was convoluted enough to confuse anyone. More than once she had been both impressed and dismayed by his cunning and cleverness.

He wiped the back of his hand across his eyes. The wavering light made him look like he was swaying. Reaching into the tunnel entrance, he retrieved the canteen and offered her a drink. She tipped the container back and drank greedily.

He pulled the saddlebags out of the tunnel and flung them open. "You best eat something." He dropped two hard biscuits and a piece of jerky in her lap.

She stared at the food. Never before had she realized how much effort it took to move her head. The food had all the appeal of two rocks and a scrap of leather, and she made no move to pick it up.

"You'll sleep better if your stomach ain't barkin' to be fed."

She lifted her gaze to him again, fascinated by the way his face floated. She wanted to lift her hand and pin it in place, but couldn't make her limbs obey.

"Eat." He commanded, nodding in her direction as he bit his biscuit in half.

She lifted her hand and stared vacantly at a biscuit. She absently sank her teeth into the hard exterior. As she chewed and swallowed, her only thought was how much her teeth hurt.

From somewhere, an annoying voice croaked. "Bed," was the only word she understood. When she didn't respond, Brewster tugged her to her feet and pushed her toward the wooden-slatted cot. As she tumbled onto it, she had a drifting feeling that she should be worried about something, but she couldn't remember what and promised herself to think about it in the morning. She felt a coarse blanket across her shoulders.

⋆⋆

Someone was fighting close to her bed. Turning over, she pulled the covers closer, wishing the noise would go away and leave her in peace. The commotion only grew louder. Pushing herself out of sleep, she struggled through a sense of weightlessness.

"Go away," she mumbled and sank into oblivion.

A shout jolted her back to consciousness.

She awoke instantly, but nothing seemed right. It was too dark. The bed was too hard and too narrow. The blankets were scratchy. There was an earthy smell in the room. Her senses tingled with alarm.

She heard it again. The rough, fear-laced voice, the indistinguishable words. Then she remembered and bolted upright in bed, straining to see. A thin bar of gloomy light gave shape to the cut log that served as a table. She saw the remains of the candle. Gingerly, she lowered her feet to the floor and stepped over to pluck a match from the box and light the candle. The agonized mumbling continued.

Lifting the shaft of weak light, she turned slowly, fearing what she would find.

Brewster lay curled up on the floor at the foot of the bed. Suddenly, he flinched and called out in a voice that made her cringe. Holding her breath, she bent closer and saw that he was still asleep. He must be dreaming. Probably about Sam and Petey, she decided.

She grabbed his shoulder to shake him. His body recoiled away from her as though her hand had seared his flesh, and he cried out, his words plain enough for her to understand.

"Stop. Stop. I'll be good. I promise."

She held her hand above his shoulder, shivering at the fear in his voice. He sounded different. His voice was higher, almost childlike. She wondered if he was dreaming something from his childhood. She trembled as she recalled how she used to wake up crying from a dream that haunted her. In it she was running blindly down a dark hallway calling

Andrew's name. It seemed he was just out of her grasp in an open doorway that was always beyond her reach.

A shudder raced across her shoulders. Swallowing back her own shadowy terror, she grasped his arm and pulled.

Again he flinched, flailing against the wall in his attempt to avoid her. "No, Lucy. Please don't hurt me."

Nausea rolled in the pit of her stomach. Someone had hurt him. From the sound of his voice she guessed it had happened when he was a child. The thought of a child being deliberately misused triggered a rush of emotion. Suddenly she wanted to hold and comfort this man who was her captor, her enemy. But that was impossible, she reasoned. It was the child he used to be that she wanted to soothe. She pressed her fingers to her lips as her eyes welled with tears.

"I didn't mean to. You hurt me." His voice held a note of surprise and in his sleep, he touched his left cheek.

The pain in his voice tore through her. She had to find a way to waken him—to stop this awful nightmare, but when she again touched his shoulder he flung her away. She barely managed to keep the candle from being thrown across the room. Reaching out to set it on the table and taking a deep breath, she grabbed his face between her palms.

"Brewster," she shouted. "Wake up." She ducked in time to dodge his outflung arm. But she had touched his skin long enough to realize that he was burning up.

Her thoughts raced into action. Which one of his wounds was infected? How was she to examine them when he reacted so violently to the slightest touch? And how was she going to treat them? There was nothing here. Or was there? She hadn't given the room more than a bare glance last night. Was it still night?

Suddenly, the impact of his illness hit her and she sank to her heels, rubbing her chin. As soon as it was light enough, she could slip away. He was in no shape to stop her or even know she was gone. She could simply walk away.

God had answered her pleas. All day she had comforted herself with the words "I will never leave thee nor forsake thee." Assuring herself that God was with her, she trusted Him to provide a way out of this ordeal. Over and over she had prayed for a means of escape.

And now God had provided the opportunity she'd been waiting for.

But what about Brewster? Could she in good conscience leave him as he was?

Doubts nibbled at the back of her mind. Could she find her way home and, at the same time, avoid running into Petey and Sam? This thought had been the reason she blindly followed Brewster through her haze of exhaustion. But now, escape was finally possible.

She continued to kneel at Brewster's side as her thoughts played tug-of-war. What would happen to him if she left? Would he die alone except for his tortured memories?

Someone named Lucy had hurt him in the past. But why should she care about his past?

She studied him. What had he been like as a child? Did his face light with innocent anticipation or did he learn to wear that guarded look so young it had always been there? Had his lips ever softened in a smile or were they always a straight, tight line? With his high cheekbones and strongly squared jaw, she had to admit his face was handsome despite the scar. He would have been a beautiful child, she guessed. Then she remembered that he had been merely a child, five or something, when he got that scar. Was it Lucy, and not his mother, who was responsible for it? Who was Lucy and why did she hurt him? Why would anyone want to hurt an innocent child? Who was this man? Why did he cry out in his sleep like one tortured? What would drive someone to such desperate measures for companionship?

She nodded as she made up her mind. She would stay and take care of him. She would be the opposite of whoever Lucy was. And in the process, maybe she'd find the answer to some of her questions. She would pry the information from him somehow.

Remembering his habit of grunting replies, she knew it would take a lot of prodding to get what she wanted. She chuckled softly, enjoying the thought of the challenge.

She straightened. What she needed right now was some Epsom salts and hot water for compresses to draw out the infection. And maybe a strong pair of arms to hold him down. Lifting the candle, she looked around. Perhaps there was something she could use. In the corner, hanging next to the minuscule stove, were three shelves. Moving closer, she peered at the contents. There was the usual collection of tin dishes and a half-dozen books. *How odd,* she thought, *for someone to leave books in a hovel like this.* Next to the books was a small, square box. Pulling it out, she discovered an assortment of items—shoe hook, needle case, a small screwdriver, a pair of scissors—*some sort of survival kit,* she thought, but nothing to meet her present needs.

Then she spied a bottle far back on the top shelf. Straining forward on her tiptoes, she reached for it, catching it as her fingers tipped it forward. A cork had been jammed into the mouth. She tried to pry it free as Brewster's ramblings continued. With a low growl, she bit the cork and jerked it free. It smelled like a home-brewed remedy and the eye-watering fumes convinced her that the contents were powerful enough to kill any infection.

Returning to his side, she stared down at his restless body, wondering how she would manage to examine him. Setting the bottle and candle at a safe distance, she knelt beside him, gritting her teeth as she grasped his shirt sleeve. With a garbled protest, he pulled away. She pressed her hands to her thighs and considered her options. Ignoring the way her insides twisted and turned, she grabbed his hand and pinned it under her knees.

"No, Lucy. No," he muttered over and over while she checked the wound on his arm. His agonized words forged a deep ache in her heart.

She poured some of the vile liquid on his wound and

flinched as he cried out. Tearing a strip from her already ragged petticoat, she sponged the wound and bound it.

The injury on his arm didn't appear to be deep. She doubted it would send him into fevered delirium. Her worry burgeoned. Amid his protests and mumblings, she released his hand. Immediately, he scuttled backward until he was pressed into the wall.

She watched, knowing the wound on his head would take a great deal more effort to check than had the arm. How could she restrain him? She considered her few options and she shrank back before each one. But having cast her lot in one direction, she determined to follow through even if it meant doing things she found distasteful. Gritting her teeth, she swung her leg over his chest, pinning him as best she could.

"I'm not going to hurt you, Brewster," she murmured, hoping her voice would break through his confusion and either comfort him or jolt him out of his ramblings.

Arching his back, he fell silent as though aware that another being had intruded into his delirium. Abby held her breath, waiting to see if he would calm.

"No," he grunted and heaved his body to the side. She braced her hands against the wall and tightened her leg muscles, but her weight was useless against his strength and she fell to the floor as he continued to protest.

There had to be another way, she determined as she pulled herself to a squat. Hesitating but a moment, she edged around until she faced his head, being careful not to touch him. Murmuring what she hoped were comforting sounds, she positioned one knee on either side of his head, still avoiding any contact. Waiting until he seemed a bit calmer, she clamped his head between her knees.

"Now hold still," she ordered in her firmest voice. It seemed to work better than her soft words.

She grabbed the candle and bent to examine his head. The odor was enough to tell her the wound was infected. Except for the spots matted with blood, his hair was as straight and heavy as the fringes on an altar cloth. *So unlike my flyaway curls,* she thought with a touch of resentment.

The wound looked like something the dog had dragged around for days and buried a few times. She wished she had checked it yesterday. Then, shrugging, she admitted she had given his injuries no more than a passing thought as the terror of escaping Sam and Petey had consumed her. Hoping she could make up for her neglect, she lifted the bottle and poured on the pungent liquid, gripping her knees as hard as she could as he tried to pull away from the pain. She used another piece of her rapidly shrinking petticoat to clean it. Her knees growing weaker by the minute, she hurried to pour on more disinfectant. Setting the candle a safe distance away, she shifted her weight to her cramped feet and pushed herself up and quickly stepped away. Brewster murmured a protest and lay still.

She brushed her skirt and felt the warmth inside her knees. He was as hot as a washday fire and she knew if she hoped to see him recover, she had to fight the fever. Pouring a cupful of their precious supply of water into a pan, she added a couple of shots from the jug. With nothing else to use, she tore yet another strip from what remained of her petticoat. Dampening the rag, she knelt beside him, wondering if he would fight like a mad bull. Taking a deep breath, she prepared to duck his flailing arms.

"Lie still," she ordered as she leaned forward. Again, at the sound of her loud words, he tensed but lay still. She ran her rag over his brow and down his cheek. He lifted his chin and turned toward her. *Like a kitten,* she thought, as tenderness swept through her like a wind. She choked back a yearning to stroke his cheek; a great hunger consumed her innards making her long to weep.

She shook her head in vigorous denial. *He kidnapped me,* she reminded herself. *All I care about is getting away from him. Just as soon as he's well again. I don't feel anything for him but dislike.* Her fingertips burned as she pressed them to her face and she plunged them into the tepid water. It took several seconds for her breathing to return to normal and her heart to stop its erratic pounding.

It's because I'm so tired, she assured herself. Tired of running for her life. Tired of riding up and down. She was plain and simple tired. That's why she'd reacted to his nuzzling the way she had. *That and a bit of pity,* she admitted. Pity for his pain, both present and past.

six

Dusty gray light filtered through the room and tickled her nose as her thoughts drifted peacefully like floating dust mites. A muffled grunt slid across her soft wakenings, but it was only an annoying interruption and she curled tighter and let the lazy drifting continue. Her back was cold and she snuggled closer to the warmth in front of her.

A sound—half-grunt, half-growl—snapped her eyes open. She found herself staring into Brewster's dark, watchful eyes just inches away.

"My goodness," she mumbled as she bolted upright. Intense heat flooded her cheeks.

Brewster never blinked, but his eyes grew more wary.

"I must have dozed off," she murmured, her voice thick with deep thirst and not enough sleep. Then she remembered why she was at his side. "How are you feeling?" She cleared her throat as the words stuck.

"Fine." Another grunt.

She pressed a hand to his brow. "You're still hot." She leaned over him to stare at his head wound. His eyes never left her. Unwilling to meet his questioning eyes, she studied the wound. "You were raving last night."

She sat back to see his reaction.

He never blinked, but behind his eyes she saw something dark and unfathomable.

"Who's Lucy?" she asked.

The lines around his mouth deepened. He didn't answer.

"Is she someone from your childhood?"

He turned to stare at the ceiling, his jaw clenching and unclenching. "She's my mother."

"Your mother!" She had thought. . .she didn't know what

she'd expected, but not his mother.

"What did I say?" His voice had dropped to a low rumble.

"Not much," she stammered, but his words rang through her head like stabbing accusations. *Stop. I'll be good. Please don't hurt me.* She choked back the bitter taste in the back of her throat. She couldn't look at him. Leaping to her feet, she stumbled across the room to pour water into the chipped enamel basin. She plunged the rag into the water, letting her hands spend several minutes swishing back and forth. One burning question blazed across her mind, demanding an answer. She tried to ignore it as she scrunched down next to Brewster and sponged his brow. He closed his eyes, his mouth tight and lipless, the tiny lines around his eyes deepening in pain. Perhaps, she thought, it was only her own distress magnifying what she saw. She wanted to cry out, to protest what he had said. But could she deny it when she suspected he spoke the truth?

Pus still seeped at the edges of the gash on his head, but it seemed less than before.

"Did your mother hurt you?" She paused long enough to watch his reaction but she didn't need eyes to know she had stunned him. A shudder rippled through him.

"She tried," he muttered, his words almost lost in the depths of his soul.

"Why?" she demanded. "Why would a mother try to hurt her child?" Confusion clouded her mind. "Were you difficult?" She knew that wouldn't make it right.

He flung her away and glowered at her. "I was not 'difficult,' as you say." He chewed out the words like they were full of sand. "I never did anything to deserve what I got." He fell back, crossing his arms, his chin protruding in stubborn defiance.

She couldn't speak, her mind was a bog of sticky confusion of what-ifs and whys and it just couldn't be. Suddenly, she realized how slack jawed she was and clamped her mouth shut, blinking as she tried to sort things out. Her eyes focused on the scar on his left cheek. It flared its way into her thoughts.

It was the only concrete thing she could find.

He saw her look at his cheek.

"If I hadn't learned to duck and run, she would have killed me. This," he jabbed his finger at his scar, "is my punishment for not paying attention."

"No." She shook my head. He was surely mistaken. Children don't always see things the way they are. It must have been an accident. He just misunderstood. She could imagine his mother—Lucy—trying to console her son, weeping and begging forgiveness, and Brewster, so stubborn and hard, refusing to grant it. "You must be wrong."

He glared at her a minute longer then turned to study the ceiling. "I was watching the dust flecks dance in a bar of sunlight." His voice was a flat monotone and she thought he was talking about the air above them. Then he continued, in the same dead voice, like a child reciting a poem that made no sense to him. "The sunlight crawled up the wall and landed on a pile of crates. I climbed up to see where it went but the stack tipped over, making a horrible racket. I hurried to the corner, but Lucy's friend came crashing through the door and saw me. I remember how he shrugged into his braces and then smacked them in place. I thought it was strange that his boots were unlaced.

" 'This kid yours?' he bellowed.

"Lucy was standing in the doorway, begging him to come back.

" 'What kind of woman are ya, locking a little kid in this rat hole while you fool around next door?' Then he pushed her away and stomped out.

"I tried to shrink into the corner, hoping I could become invisible, but she grabbed me. She lifted my feet off the ground as she shook me. I kept waving my toes hoping to touch the floor, hoping maybe I could break loose.

" 'I curse the day you was borned,' she screamed. 'Too bad you didn't die.'

"And she threw me into the crates.

"I caught my cheek on a nail."

Abby's chest felt trapped under a heavy stone. His flat, tone-less voice did nothing to dispel her horror. She moved her mouth but no words came out. There were no words. Her mind was black, swirling denial. It wasn't possible for a mother to act that way. Mothers were kind and gentle and pro-tective. She remembered something her aunt Aggie had said about a mother being more protective than a bear with cubs.

"But she couldn't have felt that way all the time," Abby protested.

"She hated me." There was no anger or self-pity in his voice. He could have been saying, "Today is Monday."

"There must have been times when she showed you love."

"Never."

Had he never known what it was to be touched with affec-tion? That would explain a lot of things. "Is that why you flinch when I touch you?"

He turned, his eyes flaring with denial. "I don't. . ." His voice trailed off. "It wouldn't work, would it?"

"What?"

"Me trying to be a husband."

"What on earth do you mean?" What did Lucy's treatment have to do with getting married?

"I thought it would be better if I had someone to talk to." She could hear his loud swallow. "I thought a woman would— if I had a wife it would be different. But I know nothing about loving and touching."

She heard the defeat in his voice and wanted to protest that he had to give love a chance. She swallowed back a stubborn lump in her throat. How could she? She didn't want to offer him love. She wanted to go home and forget this had hap-pened. "Has no one ever shown you love?" Surely there had been someone in his life who had seen the little boy and known his need.

He closed his eyes as if trying to remember—or was he trying to forget?

"Love?" He snorted. "I don't believe in it."

She was flung back into confusion. "What do you believe in?"

Slowly, as if turned by a distant force, he turned and stared into her face, his eyes hollow and haunted.

"I don't believe in anything." His words echoed the emptiness of his eyes.

A swirling abyss hovered between them. She wanted to shake him. Slap him. Hug him. She didn't know what she wanted except to prove him wrong. He had to believe in something. Especially love. God loved him. He had to know that. He had to believe it. But when she opened her mouth to speak the words that were hammering in her brain, his eyes glistened and silently denied everything she believed in.

"Seems to me you have to decide to accept love and kindness instead of kicking and snapping when people offer it to you." She saw him recoil at her harsh words, but she was too angry to withdraw them.

"You offering it to me?" His voice was low. When she didn't answer he continued. "I thought not. Words come easy, don't they? Besides, what would you know? What's the worst thing that ever happened to you?"

"Apart from this little episode?" She paused long enough to see him furrow his forehead, then she hurried on, determined to prove him wrong. "I thought you knew all about me."

He snorted. "Not much. Just that you and Andrew are twins and come from the old country."

"Well, if you must know, my mother died when I was two. But I suppose I couldn't classify that as a deep sorrow. I barely remember her except. . ." She had never told anyone—not even Andrew—of the fleeting memory she clung to. But something in Brewster's expression—a flicker that departed as quickly as it came—made her want to prove to him that all mothers—all women—were not the same.

"I remember being held on her lap, and feeling her heart against my cheek. I sometimes think I can hear her humming a song—perhaps a lullaby." So easily she slipped back into her comforting memory. She blinked her eyes and focused again on Brewster. His eyes narrowed and the shutters fell back in place, yet he watched her intently. She plucked at the hem of her skirt. "I guess I never really missed her because I couldn't really remember her. Father and Andrew were always there."

"So no unhappy memories."

"Just a brief one." Again, she hesitated. It seemed so trivial compared to what he had allowed her to see of his past, yet at the time she had been devastated. His eyes compelled her to continue. "It was when we started school. The teacher thought it would be good for Andrew and me to be separated, so she put us in different classes. I wasn't even supposed to see him during school hours. I thought my world had dumped me upside down and left me hanging. I wept bitterly. I couldn't eat and if Father forced me to, I threw it all back up again. I don't know what happened to change things. I suppose Father went to the teacher and reasoned with her. Anyway, we were allowed to be together for our classes. After that, I found I liked school." She couldn't look at him, knowing he would surely mock her little bit of trouble. And she couldn't blame him. Yet even now her stomach knotted and kicked at the thought of not being able to see Andrew. Where was he? Was he looking for her? She was sure he would be, but how would he know where to look?

"Is that why you've never married?"

His question brought her back with a thud and she stared at him. "What?"

"You're too dependent on Andrew. It keeps you from other relationships."

She stumbled to her feet, fighting an urge to throw the basin of water in his face. "How dare you make such a mean accusation! Andrew and I are very close but that does not keep us from living a normal life."

His expression never altered. Her impassioned response meant no more to him than the anger of an ant.

"Is he as dependent on you?"

"Of course. I mean of course not." He quirked his eyebrows mockingly. "Oh, you're despicable." Her innards twisted like a ride on a bucking horse. "Andrew has always been protective of me. We share everything. He's very kind and patient." She stopped. Why had she said patient? It sounded like she was a pest but Andrew put up with her. It made her sound demanding. Was she demanding? Was she dependent? After all, they were twins—motherless twins. But was it unhealthy? Had she kept Andrew from pursuing his own life? Did he wish for freedom? She thought of the few girlfriends he'd had and tried to remember whether any of them had visited more than once or twice. She could think of only two who had come to the house three times. Was she the reason?

She leaned forward as pain pierced upward from the pit of her stomach. She would do anything rather than be the cause of hurting Andrew. Out of her turmoil, she saw Brewster, who had flung these darts of doubt into her life. She turned on him, her chin jutting forward. "It's you that has sick emotions. You see the world through a cracked glass. Don't try to make my world look as sick as yours. Andrew and I are twins. Our love is special."

"What would I know?" He shrugged and looked away. "I know nothing about love."

It wasn't the response she wanted. She preferred accusations and arguments to being faced with his disbelief in love. "Listen, God loves you."

"How convenient!" His eyes flared with accusation. "No one else loves you, but God does. What is He, the universal dump for unlovable souls? You should make a banner for Him. 'Apply here for handouts. Only the dregs of society accepted.' "

She wanted to shout a denial, but his words burned into her heart. It was too close to what she had been thinking and she felt a sting in the back of her throat. "It isn't that way, Brewster."

"How is it then? No kid should ever have to go through

what I did. Where was God then?"

She shrank from the pain and anger in his voice even as she realized it was the first time he had allowed himself to express his emotion. Somehow she had to convince him that God did care in spite of what he'd experienced. "He must have sent you someone who showed a little kindness."

"You could also say He sent me Bubba."

"Bubba?"

"Yeah. The guy who beat me until I couldn't walk."

"No. I don't think you can blame God for Bubba. God is a God of love and I know He hates that sort of thing. I'm sure there's a hotter place in hell for people like Bubba."

"Bubba was just a drunk. He wasn't a mother." His emotions had drained him and he turned away, his voice back to the flat rumble she'd grown used to.

"Not all mothers are like Lucy."

"How would you know? You never had a mother."

He was as determined to refuse to believe in love as she was to prove it. "Brewster, would you know love if you had it? Would you accept it?"

He closed his eyes and didn't answer. She placed the basin on the table and went to the saddlebags. There were still a few hard biscuits and some jerky. Hardly enough to see them through another day. Where would this day take them? She turned to ask Brewster, but his mouth was slack and his face soft. He had fallen asleep.

He slept long and sound.

She took a book from the shelf and lay on the bed but couldn't get interested in reading "Essays" by someone called Ralph Waldo Emerson. She put the book back and searched the other titles but none of them caught her fancy. Restless, she circled the room, peering out the narrow slit of a window set into a deep, earthen wall, but all she could see was a patch of blue. A heavy robe had been pulled over the tunnel entrance. Brewster must have done that last night to keep the draft out. Beside the cupboards she had examined during the

night, there was only a narrow door about four feet high. A
closet, she assumed. She pulled on the leather strap. It stuck.
She braced her feet and heaved. Reluctantly it opened, a gush
of fresh air sweeping across the room. A short tunnel opened
to the outside. Glancing over her shoulder, she saw that
Brewster remained asleep. He would be okay now. She could
leave with a clear conscience. Gathering up the blanket from
the bed, she stuffed four dry biscuits into her pocket.
Tiptoeing across the dirt-packed floor, she ducked through
the door and pulled it shut behind her.

Five crouching steps took her to freedom and she filled her
lungs, stretching as she studied the surroundings for a familiar landmark. Below her lay a wide, green valley. Nothing
looked familiar about the trees or the lay of the land. The
mountains lay so close it seemed she could reach out her
hand and touch them, but the peaks and rocky slopes were
foreign. She searched the rising skyline for some point of ref-
erence, but there was nothing.

A cold wind shivered down her spine and she spun around
to study the sky. Far to her left rolled a black thundercloud,
breathing out ice and fear. Lighting flashed and, seconds
later, thunder bounced back and forth across the valley.
Before she could assess the strength of the storm, the sky
grew as dark as a winter's evening. Abby began to shiver.
The sun ducked behind the mountains, fingering the sky. The
storm was about to break.

A cold shudder shook her shoulders. Nature was against
her escape. Common sense overcame her urge for freedom
and she retraced her steps to the doorway. It had latched
behind her and in the dark she could feel no way to open it.
Forcing herself to take a deep breath, she examined the door
again and with shaking fingers found a bit of protruding
wood. Yanking upward, she felt it release. She put her shoulder to the door, heaved it open, and stumbled into the room,
kicking the door shut behind her to block the rush of cold air.

Brewster grunted and opened his eyes as the blast of cold

hit him. His eyes met hers. "Look what the wind blew in," he muttered.

Self-consciously, she raked her fingers through her hair, knowing it was tangled beyond repair. Not everyone could have smooth heavy hair like his, she fumed, replying, "You look a bit sorry at the edges too."

"Feel about the same." There was no rancor in his voice. He started to get to his feet, but grabbed his head and fell back with a moan. When he opened his eyes and looked at her, she could see they were dark with pain. "I could sure use a drink," he whispered.

Sighing, she took him the canteen, steadying it as he pulled it to his mouth and drained the last of it. He fell asleep immediately. She knew it was a healing sleep. With a glance at the closed door, she wondered if he would recover before she could escape.

Crossing the room to the tunnel they had entered the night before, she checked the other canteen, letting her breath out through pursed lips when she discovered it was almost full. Turning, she retraced her steps, rubbing her arms as she paced. The room had grown cool and she wrapped the blanket around her shoulders and stood before the cold stove, toying with the idea of starting a fire. Would the smoke give away their hiding place? Was it possible Sam and Petey still stalked them? She knew they weren't the type to give up easily but the damp coldness seemed to burrow into her bones. She glanced at Brewster but he continued to sleep. She knew at a glance his fever had broken, but lying on the cold, earthen floor was certainly unhealthy, she reasoned. Before she could think better of it, she dropped the blanket, and grabbed a handful of wood to shove in the firebox. She promised herself she'd keep the fire low. Just enough heat to warm her bones. The kindling caught immediately. She leaned over the first flames, waiting for the heat. It felt so good. She turned and warmed her back. The warm flow of blood in her veins was invigorating. She gathered together the meager ingredients, combining what the saddlebags and shelves had to offer, and mixed up johnnycake. As it baked, she rationed out enough water for two cups of tea.

The fire had burned to flickering embers when Brewster raised his head, pressing a hand to his wound and growled, "Smoke. I smell smoke."

"I fired up the stove," she explained.

He sat up and braced his hands on the floor. His eyes rolled and he swayed, but he gritted his teeth and remained upright. "Sam and Petey will smell it. They'll find us in no time."

"Don't worry. It's raining out. They'll be holed up somewhere trying to keep dry." She picked up a plate of still-warm corn bread smothered in molasses, and poured the boiling water over the tea. "This will make you feel better." She held the plate and cup toward him.

He stared at her without taking the plate, then shook his head and moaned as the movement brought pain. "I hope you're right, but with their type I've learned never to assume anything."

"I was pretty close to Sam and I think it's fairly safe to assume he has an aversion to water." She wrinkled her nose in remembrance.

He didn't smile. He never smiled. But the lines around his eyes deepened and he snorted softly. It was enough for Abby and she grinned at him, pleased at his reaction.

He sank back to his elbows and took a bite of food. "Good," was all he said but she was gratified.

He cleaned his plate and again slept. She blew out the candle and lay down on the cot.

It was dark when she woke to the sound of Brewster moving about.

"Hey," he whispered gruffly. "Let's go."

She startled awake in the cold. "Go?"

"Hurry. Let's get out of here."

She staggered to her feet and followed him blindly, barely able to make out his outline as they slipped through the door.

The sky was steel, revealing the faint outline of the two horses, saddled and waiting. Abby blinked as she realized she had slept while he moved about and saddled horses. A burning anger watered her eyes. She had slept through her chance to escape. How could she continue to ask God to help when she failed to take advantage of the opportunities He sent? Now it was too late. She was stuck having to again follow Brewster. But until another chance came along, Brewster was preferable to being in the hands of Sam and Petey. She swung into the saddle without protest.

As they traversed the hill, she called to Brewster. "What is that place? How did you know it was there?"

"It's an old miner's cabin. I stumbled on it a year or so ago. I fixed it up some. I still use it once in a while."

She glanced back but the entrance had disappeared into the hillside. She turned her attention to staying on the trail.

The cold seeped through her, numbing her brain as she clung to the saddle, her horse patiently plodding after Brewster's mount. The sky turned to gray and then slowly lightened to blue, but the air was damp and did not warm in the early sunshine.

They climbed one slope and then skidded down another. Every hillside looked the same to her, and she wondered whether they were riding in circles. Once, they stopped by a pencil-thin waterfall to drink and fill their canteens.

As it grew warmer, she let the blanket slide from her shoulders. The day grew hot and sticky. She could no longer feel her legs. If only she could say the same for her back. It screamed at every rough step the horse took.

She shook herself out of her weariness as something about her new surroundings stirred her subconscious. They were in the valley now. They climbed less, and there were more deciduous trees. She twisted in the saddle to look over her shoulder. The mountains rose behind them. Her stomach churned as she tried to pinpoint the uneasiness tugging at her.

"Where are we going?" she called to the back she had

watched for hour after endless hour until she had memorized the width of his shoulders, the fringe of black hair, the narrowness of his hips.

Brewster raised a hand to signal her to keep quiet.

She swung her head back and forth as her stomach lurched against her ribs. Her neck muscles tightened. Something felt very wrong but she didn't know what it was.

Brewster reined to a halt and reached for her horse as she drew abreast.

He dismounted and she followed his lead, paying scant attention to her numb legs as she continued to study the hillside and nearby trees, her glance racing from place to place. She rubbed her breastbone as her apprehension mounted.

"Stay quiet," Brewster whispered as he led the horses into the trees and tied them.

She remained under the shelter of the trees, waiting, watching, but for what she couldn't guess.

"Come on," he growled as he returned to her side. When she didn't respond, he grabbed her hand and pulled her after him. They went about thirty steps before he dropped to his stomach on the ground, pulling her down beside him.

"What are you doing?" she demanded, as her near-panic swelled.

"Shh." He held his finger to his lips then began to edge forward. "Follow me."

She obeyed him. They crawled to the brow of a hill. Her stomach banged at her throat. She pressed her hand to her mouth as she stared down the slope at her house—Andrew's and hers. It looked just as she had left it. Somehow she had expected it to be different. Two towels flapped on the line. *They'll be bleached to snowy whiteness,* she thought and then wondered why it mattered. Two horses nibbled at the grass behind the barn. It looked like a peaceful, pastoral scene, but every nerve in her body was screaming disaster, and she twisted around to face Brewster.

"There's something wrong," she croaked.

seven

"Shh." With narrowed, intent eyes, he studied the view below them. "This could be a trap."

"No," she shook her head. "No."

She became the object of his narrow-eyed scrutiny.

"No, what?"

"It's not a trap. There's something wrong." Her words raced out in a tangle. "If I try, I can always feel Andrew, no matter how far apart we are. I can't feel him." She pressed her hand to her chest. "He's not there. He's gone." Staring at the empty yard, she choked back a wail as the ice in her innards roared into flaming anger. She turned on Brewster. "Why are we here? What are you up to? Did you do something to him?" she demanded with piercing intensity.

His eyes darkened and his expression hardened, but she ignored it. Something had happened to Andrew and it was Brewster's fault, if not directly, than indirectly.

"I was taking you back. I figured you'd be safer with Andrew than with me." His words were deep and low in his throat. "Besides, without you to watch out for, I could deal with Sam and Petey."

She instantly dismissed the fleeting pang of guilt. She couldn't reason. Panic was drowning her. She sprang to her feet and started running down the hill toward the house.

She stumbled a few feet before Brewster's arms grabbed her around the waist. She tripped and they fell to the ground.

"Let me go." She spat the words out around coarse blades of grass. She said it again as she tried to untangle herself and get up, but he held her to the ground. Finally, she lay still, hoping he would release her if she stopped fighting. He didn't move. His warm body pressed her to the ground. Her lungs ached. "Please let me go. I can't breathe."

He eased his weight back, but his arms still pressed her shoulders down.

"Please. I must find him."

"First, we make sure it's safe. No point in getting tangled in our own lariat." He uncoiled and stood over her while she scrambled to her feet. Motioning her to follow him, he edged his way down the hill.

She couldn't tell how long they took. It seemed they weren't making any progress and then, the next thing she knew, they were at the door. Brewster held her back as he eased in and checked the room. She pushed past him and dashed inside.

"Andrew," she called, her voice echoing in the empty room. She paused and listened, then dashed to her bedroom, giving it a cursory glance. She didn't need to look to know he wasn't there. She didn't need to climb the stairs to the loft where he slept. Nevertheless, she hurried upstairs. Again, the silent room stared back.

"He's not here." A bitterness burned inside her stomach. "I told you he wasn't."

"When did you expect him back from his trip?"

"The day he left. Or maybe the next if he had to drive some horses." Her eyes continued to dart across the room as if some object would give her a clue to his whereabouts. A fine layer of dust lay on the table like ashes from a cold fire. She wanted to scrub it clean, to somehow reverse the tide of events. Instead, she swiped her finger across the table, leaving a long slash in the sooty layer. She stared at her dirty fingertips.

"Maybe he took longer than he expected."

She scrubbed her hands on her skirt. "No." Her tone indicated her conviction. It wasn't as simple as Andrew having been delayed. There was something very wrong. Her gaze settled on a black, wide-brimmed hat that hung on a nail by the door. She grabbed it. "His good hat. He always wore it to town. He was wearing it when he left." Her fingers brushed the brim, remembering how careful he was to keep this hat in good repair. "No need to go to town looking poorly," he always said as he positioned it on his thick hair—coppery colored like her own, but roguishly attractive on him. It was the one thing she had begrudged him, but now she vowed that she would never again complain about him having the nicer hair, if only he would turn up safe now. She scurried to the window, knowing without looking that the yard would be empty. Beside her, the flies bounced against the window-pane, the noise threading into her ears until it boomed. She turned back to the room, noticing the horses as she spun around. "Besides, there's a bunch of horses in the pasture. He must have bought some and drove them home."

Her footsteps rang hollow as she crossed to the stove and stared at the cold kettle. Something sat uneasy in her brain. When had she first noticed his absence in her mind? She remembered feeling him looking for her the night they spent in the cave. That was almost three days ago. She couldn't remember sensing him again until they were on the hill overlooking the buildings. By then her heart was already screaming disaster.

Her insides were ready to explode. She paced back to the table, almost tripping on the laundry basket. In her mind, she pictured herself dropping it as Brewster's arm trapped her. Andrew must have brought it in when he got home and found her missing. She imagined his distress—a mirror image of her own feelings. She dropped his hat on the table and pressed her hands to her ears to block out the droning that went on and on.

Brewster made a sound deep in his throat. "Maybe we should look around outside."

She beat him to the door and ran toward the garden; then, realizing Andrew wouldn't be there, she headed toward the clothesline. The two tea towels flapped in a gust of wind, like thunder in her ears. She snatched them from the line without stopping and spun around to race toward the barn, catching up to Brewster as he pulled open the door. Stepping inside, he paused to study the surroundings. He slowly checked inside the three stalls on one side, crossed the alleyway and checked the three stalls on the other side.

Rocking back and forth on the balls of her feet, Abby shouted, "Andrew," and cocked her head to listen.

Overhead, she heard the whir of pigeons' wings.

"He's not here." She was breathless. Her tongue stuck to the bottom of her mouth.

"I tell you he's not here anywhere." Her voice rose to a wail. "We have to find him."

Brewster turned his dark, hooded eyes to her. "We?" His eyebrows shot up.

"Yes, we. After all, it's all your fault. If you hadn't. . ."

"Whoa up there, now. Guess I acted rashly, thinking I could kidnap myself a wife. It was a mistake and all, but I brought you back in the same condition as I found you. I figure that makes things square."

"Mistake. Same condition? What am I? A borrowed saw or something?"

"No, ma'am." He stood motionless, his hands dangling at his side.

"You think you can just grab some poor, unsuspecting girl and ride halfway across the country and back, make me hide in caves and scale cliffs, go cold and hungry, and then change your mind and say things are square and that makes everything fine? Is that what you think?"

"No, ma'am."

"Besides, as I said, if you hadn't kidnapped me, Andrew wouldn't have ridden out. You have to help me find him."

"Now hold on a mite." He rubbed his chin. "You don't even know if he needs finding."

She stomped her foot and blinked back tears. "I keep trying to tell you. I know he needs help. Why won't you listen?"

"Lady," he answered, looking toward the roof and shaking his head. "I am listening."

"Then you aren't hearing."

"You mean I'm not agreeing."

"Oh! Forget it." She stomped from the barn and raced across the yard to the horses tied to the hitching post. Grabbing up the reins of the horse she had ridden all day, she pulled the animal away from the rail.

Brewster stood in her way. "What are you doing?"

"What does it look like? I'm going to find Andrew. If you won't help me I'll do it alone."

"Aren't you forgetting something?"

She paused, one foot in the stirrup, but her mind was too tightly wound to be able to guess at his meaning. "What?"

"That's my horse."

"Tough." She swung herself into the saddle and grasped the reins, but Brewster reached up and grabbed the chin strap before the horse could move.

"Get off." His voice was deep and low.

Abby shook her head and kicked her heels into the horse's flanks.

Brewster grabbed her around the waist.

"Let go." She squirmed, but his hold only tightened. She barely had time to shake her feet free of the stirrups before he yanked her from the saddle and swung her down to his side.

"This horse is exhausted. He deserves a rest."

"Let me go."

"You bet."

She stumbled away, then straightened and stomped to the house, mumbling under her breath, "I'll find Andrew. Somehow. Someway. And I don't need your help. Or permission." She slammed the door behind her and marched to the table where she stood leaning against a chair. She'd go catch up one of the new horses. There had to be one that was broken. Or she could wait until Brewster was asleep and take one of his. Trouble was, Brewster didn't seem to need much sleep. Her eye caught a movement out the window. It was Brewster walking along the pasture fence, his head bent as though he were looking for something. *Probably making sure I can't take one of the horses,* she fumed and turned her back.

She'd find a way to look for Andrew if she had to walk to town to get help. Brewster probably thought her fears were silly, but she knew what she knew.

She stared at the cold stove, remembering the day, in the old country, shortly after Andrew had begun work at the mill. She had been busy making a pudding for dinner. Just as she was about to add currants to the batter, an awful feeling of pain came over her. It was so sharp she checked to see if she had cut herself. But this pain didn't touch her body. It ripped her heart. She'd called Andrew's name. Father, who had been working at his accounts, looked up and reminded her that Andrew was at work. She'd tried to explain that something had happened to him, but Father assured her she was anxious because he was away while she remained at home. He gently comforted her, saying she would get used to his absence. She didn't argue, but she knew it wasn't that.

When Andrew came home that night, his hand was wrapped in a heavy, white bandage. He had caught it on a sharp corner of a wagon he was unloading and cut it badly. When Abby asked when the accident had occurred, he had given the exact time she had felt the pain in her own being.

There were other times too. Like the time they were children and his shirt had caught on a limb as he climbed a tree, holding him suspended two feet above the ground unable to help himself. In response to his calls, Abby had looked up from her own play nearby and hurried to rescue him. Only he hadn't called for help.

The only time I've been wrong was when I didn't listen to what I felt.

She heard the door open but didn't bother to look up. She'd find Andrew, she vowed, with or without Brewster's help.

Brewster grunted. "Looks like he rode out three, maybe four days ago."

She glared at the silent stove.

"I'll go look for him." His voice was a low rumble.

She spun on her heel and grabbed her coat from the hook

next to the door. "I'm coming with you."

He stared at her long and steady. "First we sleep and get some supplies ready." He remained in the doorway, twisting his hat in his hands, feet planted squarely.

She wanted to argue about the delay, but the light was already changing, throwing long, lean shadows on the ground behind him, reflecting in his eyes, making them warmer than she'd ever seen them. She blinked away the thought, knowing it was a trick of the light. Inside, he was hard and cold. Maybe even dead. She returned her coat to the peg. "I'll make some supper," she said, turning away. Every minute of delay felt like another death. Her's. Andrew's. But she knew Brewster was right. Nothing would be gained by venturing out in the dark.

Brewster stood shadowed in the doorway, motionless and broad.

"You might as well come in." She spared him a fleeting glance.

"I'll wash up first." Before she could offer him a basin of warm water, he was at the horse trough, working the pump handle up and down. A gush of water poured forth and he splashed it over his face, spattering a golden spray around him. The warm glow stirred her heart. She slammed her mind shut and handed him a towel as he climbed the steps. His eyes met hers and flashed away.

She retreated to the stove while he continued to hover at the doorway. She could not bring herself to say "make yourself at home." She was off balance at his presence in her house. On one hand, she longed to see the end of Mr. Brewster Johnson, to be free of his dark nature and laconic speech. Yet the thought of being alone made her ears pound and her chest hurt, and she wanted to grab him with both hands and bolt him to the floor. She might not like him, she assured herself, but he knew the countryside like the back of his hand and he exuded a calm, imperturbable attitude that made the future seem less foreboding. Besides, she needed him to help her find Andrew. And that was all, she reminded herself.

Nodding toward Andrew's armchair, she said, "Sit over there." It was all she could bring herself to offer.

He dipped his head and crossed the room, perching in the chair like it had a bad smell. His gaze followed her, his eyes hooded and wary.

He expects to be treated poorly—rudely, she thought with a stab of conscience. She tightened her chest muscles. She didn't care how cruel life had been to him. She wasn't responsible for the guardedness in his eyes. She had no reason to feel guilty. Then she remembered her manners. "Feel free to read the magazines." It was the neighborly thing to do. She was prepared to be polite and neighborly but nothing more.

She turned her back on him and began to peel the basin of potatoes. *God,* she silently prayed, *be with Andrew wherever he is. Keep him safe.* A sudden hollowness in her chest sucked away her breath. If anything happened to Andrew— she couldn't think about it. Brewster was right in a sense when he said she was dependent on Andrew. But it wasn't in the twisted, unhealthy way he had made it seem. It was a bond of mutual love. And a closeness that came not only of being twins but having been motherless and looking to each other to supply that lack.

The rattle of paper brought her back to her task. The first potato was still in her hand, forgotten as she stared out the window. She forced her attention to supper preparations, finishing the potatoes and putting them to boil.

As she fried the salt pork, the smell clogging her nostrils, she glanced toward Brewster. His head bent over the paper, he seemed wholly concentrated on his reading.

A few minutes later, she placed the serving bowls on the table. "Supper's ready," she said, pointing toward a chair.

He closed the magazine and rose silently, his gaze sweeping past her to the table. They pulled their chairs to place like a pair of silent actors.

Taking a quick breath, she silently thanked God for the

food. In the same breath she prayed for Andrew's safety.

"Help yourself." Her words dropped like pennies into the stillness as she handed him the platter of meat. Their eyes met. His didn't quite catch the light. It was like looking into the depths of the cave they had shared. What was he thinking? Was he regretting his decision to stay and look for Andrew? Was he wishing he had ridden out while it was still light? Did he find their closeness as nerve tingling as she did? She forced her attention to her own plate, filling her fork with fluffy mashed potatoes, but the food tasted like paper and her throat closed shut. She almost gagged. Taking a deep breath, she forced herself to swallow. The silence had become an unwelcome guest. She knew she would scream if she didn't drive it away.

"You seem to know this tracking business very well." Polite social noises were better than the breathing silence.

"I had a good teacher."

"Who was that?" Anything to stop her thoughts from leaping back and forth between silently calling Andrew, and wishing there was a way to get a better look at Brewster's eyes.

"He was a half-breed. Used to scout for the Mounties before he signed on with the cattle outfit I was with. I watched him lots. Asked a few questions and learned a pile about reading signs." He kept his head down, stabbing the meat with his fork.

Abby would not let herself admit she was disappointed that he didn't look up. "Was that a long time ago?"

"I was just a kid."

He lifted his head. *Success!* She squirmed at the dark brittleness in his eyes, uncertain as to what it meant. Was he challenging her to probe further or fighting another painful memory? There was a power in his eyes she couldn't look away from.

"How old were you?" The darkness shifted, grew less guarded yet more intense. She couldn't be certain, but she thought she detected sorrow in his expression.

"Maybe twelve."

She blinked, breaking the spell. Did he say twelve? "What

were you doing on a cattle drive at twelve?" For a heart-rending moment, she caught a glimpse in his eyes of the lonely child he had been, finding an old scout his only company. Her heart held its breath as she slid toward—stop. She reined herself in. The shutters closed and she knew a pang of loss as if she had almost discovered something supremely important.

"It was a job."

"I suppose." She kept her attention on her plate, waiting for her lungs to stop galloping about and fill with air. "I'll clean up." Gathering the dishes, she took them to the washbasin.

Later, after she had shown Brewster the ladder to Andrew's loft and he had taken a lamp and climbed the steps, she closed the door to her own room.

Overhead the floorboards creaked. A muffled thud was followed by rustling noises—all sounds she'd heard before. When it was Andrew, they were comforting—a lullaby that drifted her to sleep; but now, they were different. She lay awake, staring at the ceiling, aware of the sigh of the ceiling above her every time Brewster moved. His scent, his movements, his presence dominated the place, seeping through the pores of the house, tingling her nerves until she lay rigid as a piece of glass. *I'm being silly. Why should I be so conscious of him. We've already spent four nights together.*

But, a niggling voice answered, *those nights were out in the open. Not in your own house. And you didn't have a choice. But now he's upstairs at your invitation.*

She'd practically insisted he sleep in Andrew's bed.

I should have let him sleep out in the barn like he suggested, she thought, flipping to her side and squeezing her eyes shut.

Then the shifting above her ended and all she heard was the wind moaning around the eaves calling Andrew's name to her. The sound drilled into her heart until she pulled the covers over her head and murmured a prayer. *Lord, wherever he is, whatever's the matter, guard him and lead us to him. Keep him safe. Keep him safe. Lord, keep us all safe.*

eight

Abby shifted in the saddle, twisting and arching her back, trying to ease the stiffness. All morning she had been leaning into the day. It had been a hurry-up-and-wait day as Brewster meticulously studied the signs, examining each blade of grass, each rock, each leaf with total concentration. He was so intense that she imagined him magnifying every item until the tiniest detail spoke its history. She watched him now, down on one knee, studying the grass inch by inch. Then he straightened and looked into the distance.

When they had started out, Abby had repeatedly asked him what he saw. Could he tell if Andrew had been this way? He had merely shaken his head and continued to look. After a few rounds of questions with no answers, however, Abby discovered that, if she was quick enough to catch the expressions that flitted across his features, she could read the answers in his face. If he saw something helpful, there would be a flicker in his eyes, so tiny and brief that at first she thought she had imagined it, but it was there. When he failed to find something that he seemed to be expecting, his eyebrows would arch upward—again, almost imperceptibly—as if surprised that the clue wasn't there. When the trail would seem to grow cold, Brewster would study the ground with such intensity that Abby expected to see the grass at his feet smolder. Constantly watching him to read his expressions gave Abby plenty of opportunity to study him. And to think.

To keep her mind from its endless twisting, she tried to guess where Andrew was. The scenes she imagined were not comforting. Maybe he accidentally ran into Petey and Sam and they had taken out their frustrations on him. Or maybe this wasn't his trail at all. What if he didn't go this way at all but rode into town for help or was miles the other way?

Yesterday, his disappearance had filled her with boiling fear; but today, she suddenly realized, even with her "what-ifs" she was less frightened. Today it was more an urgency. As if she knew they would find him and the sooner the better. She examined this feeling. Why was she more determined and less panicked today? Was if because her gut—the same belly-deep feeling that assured her Andrew was not at the house—was assuring her he was at the end of the trail? Had her faith in God grown to give her a resting confidence in His love and power? She knew God would take care of Andrew and it did help her to stay calm. Or—she tried to stop the thought from blooming—was it Brewster that accounted for her calmness? Was she so trusting of his ability and willingness to help that it eased her mind?

Something between them had changed. She couldn't quite put her finger on what it was, nor was she sure she wanted to. No, that wasn't quite true. She was sure she didn't want to know. It was bad enough that she had to depend on him right now. Bad enough that she had to watch his expression like a hawk. It meant she had no choice but to see the way his eyes captured the blue of the sky or the green of the forest. It was inevitable that she would notice the way the sun caught the planes of his face, reminding her of the strength of the granite cliff they had traversed three days ago. She couldn't avoid noticing the way the breeze trickled through his hair at the back of his neck as he bent over.

He straightened in the saddle and she blinked, chasing back her thoughts, half expecting he would face her and read her mind. Her cheeks warmed with a blush, but instead of turning her way, he looked toward the west.

"What? What do you see?" She had stayed back, knowing she could destroy clues, now she urged the horse toward him.

"I've found tracks that might be his. He seems to be headed in that direction." He pointed toward the rising hills that gave way to the towering mountains and heavy forest. Abby didn't remember the exact place they had spent the first night or how they got there, but she did know they had been up in high country. She recalled the thick pine forest and the crisp air. Was Andrew headed the same direction? How would he know? She voiced her questions.

"Maybe he heard you calling him." Brewster gave her a fleeting glance before he resumed studying the land ahead of them, but it was enough for her to see his eyes were as green as the dark forest and as full of secrets. However, she had seen no hint of mockery in his eyes.

"Maybe." She ducked her head, not knowing what to think. No one had ever believed she and Andrew had this connection. Even Andrew, his intuitive awareness less intense than Abby's, doubted the depth of it. That Brewster might accept it made him seem almost likable. She didn't want to like him. This was the man who had kidnapped her, tied her wrists, subjected her to attack by two depraved men. Not only that, he was a man with deep hurts who didn't much trust other people, and women in particular. Besides, she didn't want a man. She and Andrew intended to build their new farm together.

Brewster swung into his saddle and rode silently and slowly ahead of her, leaning over his horse, ever studying the trail. He reined in. "Look. Whoever it was got off his horse here."

Even Abby could see the broken blades of grass.

Again, they followed the faint trail.

Brewster stopped. Pushing his hat back on his head, he stared at the mountains, his eyes dark, lines of concentration deepening around his mouth.

"What's wrong?" She couldn't stop the spear of alarm flashing through her insides.

"Nothing, I guess." He rubbed the back of his neck.

"Then what are you worrying about?"

He flashed her a stinging look. "I'm not worried. I'm thinking." He paused. "I'm concerned."

Abby's gaze swept over the countryside. For the first time, she noticed twisting, black thunderheads forming far to the south. A chill wind drove through her shoulder blades. "The storm?" She couldn't keep the thread of fear from lacing her voice. Even a frank greenhorn like her knew that rain would erase the faint trail they were following. For a moment she resented the frequent showers that poured over the mountains and bathed the land. Knowing that her frustration was futile, she took a deep, steadying breath.

He nodded, his eyes searching her face. "That. And something else."

It was as if he was measuring her ability to be told the truth.

"What else?" Her voice was brisk. Whatever it was, knowing was better than guessing.

"For some reason, whoever made this trail broke into a gallop about here."

She clung to his gaze, drinking from the cool depths. "What does that mean?"

He shrugged. Their eyes held like clasped children's hands. "Can't say for sure but I'd guess he saw something. Perhaps a rider. Or a fire." The way his voice deepened on the last words, Abby knew he was thinking that Andrew—if indeed it were Andrew—had seen a fire. But what fire? They'd had a small fire the first night, but it was so small and so deep in the woods she was certain it would have given no sign. The second night they had hidden in the cave. There had been no fire. "Sam and Petey. They had a fire."

"Yup. Could be that's what he saw. He'd have no way of knowin' if it was us or someone else."

She rubbed her chin then pressed her hand to her chest. "If he rode up unannounced, they might—" She choked.

"No telling what they might do. Or if he reached their camp. There's a number of obstacles between here and the mountains."

She shivered at the way he said "obstacles," but before she

could press him for an explanation, he cast an eye on the approaching storm and kicked his horse. Talk would have to wait. They had to move fast to beat the rain.

They kept up a steady lope, one that jarred Abby's spine like a hammer. They slowed only enough for Brewster to check the trail by leaning over his horse, then they resumed the jolting pace. Abby clenched her teeth, but not for anything would she call out. She had seen how the lines around Brewster's mouth deepened each time he slowed down. Something had him worried. Something more than what he told her. Her own mouth felt like it was gouged into brittle cheeks. The sound of distant thunder shuddered up her spine and she glanced over her shoulder to see black clouds churning toward them.

Their path had been as straight as a taut rope in the direction of the granite-faced mountain. Brewster called over his shoulder. "Looks for sure he was leather bent in that direction. We'll pick up the trail again when we get to the trees. Let's ride."

She didn't need any urging and clung to the saddle horn as they raced across the meadow.

Brewster leaped from his horse and grabbed her reins as she skidded to a stop. He pulled the horses into the trees and loosened their saddles before he tied them.

"Come on," he urged her, grabbing the saddlebags and canteen. "Let's find shelter." Already the first drops of rain were falling.

"What about Andrew?"

"It's only a summer storm. It will pass quickly."

He'll get soaked. She didn't say the words aloud. She breathed a prayer for Andrew—one in a long chain of petitions she had sent to her heavenly Father—then followed Brewster deeper into the trees.

"This will do." He sat on a log.

She perched beside him. Shrugging out of his batlike slicker, he reached behind her. She jumped as his arm brushed her back.

"I'm just trying to keep you dry," he growled, draping his slicker over them both. She huddled inside the damp warmth of it, holding it close with one hand, forced to crowd next to him so that they could both enjoy the protection of his coat.

She watched him open the saddlebags and noticed for the first time how long and slender his hands were and how deeply browned—almost stained looking—they were from work and weather. One fingernail was blackened and his knuckles were scraped. Likely from his fight with Sam and Petey, she guessed and wondered how much discomfort this adventure had caused him. Punched. Shot. Sick. He'd never said a word about the gunshot wound to his arm and she hadn't seen it since the night he was raving. He removed his hat to hunker under the slicker and now she studied his head wound. A blackish scab puckered at the edges. It looked nasty, but was healing well enough. Her eyes lowered to study his face. *It is so strong.* She knew he hated his scar. He said it made him ugly, but as far as she could tell, it only served to make his face stronger.

Brewster pulled some biscuits from the saddlebags, straightened, and turned to her. Their looks collided. Neither of them turned away.

She could swim in his eyes, she decided. They were so deep. Was she swimming? Or drowning? Drowning should be a violent struggle, not a gentle, swaying seduction of warmth and boneless limbs.

The lines around his mouth softened to whispers. His lips parted, revealing even white teeth like pearls of pleasure. She half lifted one hand, longing to run her fingers across his lips, to learn them by heart. She leaned toward him as his head began a slow descent. He was going to kiss her and she welcomed the thought, though the admission was dredged from a place beyond logic and reason.

A crash of thunder made her bolt to a rigid posture. She shook her head. What was she thinking? She was here for one purpose, to find her twin. She wanted only one thing from

Brewster—to help her find Andrew. She shuddered as a bolt of lightening shattered the sky and thunder roared across the land. It was the sheer force of the storm that made her heart pound in her ears. Or so she told herself.

Brewster's face was tipped to the sky, his eyes flashing. "Just listen to that thunder roll."

She'd never before seen anyone who liked a thunderstorm, but as the rain cascaded from the leaves in a hundred miniature waterfalls and the wind purred in the treetops, she watched him breathe in its majesty. The earthy aura of mushrooms and wet leaves swelled from the forest floor, mingling with the metallic scent of lightning. The aroma of pine needles, damp canvas, and sweat teased Abby's nostrils. She'd never be able to smell pine again without thinking of Brewster. A chill wind caught at the edge of the slicker. Brewster grabbed it and pulled it closer. Warmth flared into flame, searing through her being, licking at her reason, scorching her ability to think.

Thunder clapped again, reverberating through her senses, making her want to press her hands to her ears. She couldn't breathe. Her lungs grew tighter and she squeezed her eyes shut. The thunder rolled into the distance, growing farther and farther away.

The storm ended as suddenly as it had begun, sunshine back-lighting the final drops of water. The air freshened and she could breathe again. Opening her eyes, she glanced at Brewster's profile, and saw his face still upturned to the elements of nature. She was astonished to realize he was oblivious to her turmoil.

As they gathered up their things, her mind tangled in a web of unfamiliar thoughts and feelings. She slipped out of the protection of his slicker, pulling her own jacket closer around her shoulders.

She waited for him to tighten the cinch on each saddle, glad that his attention was away from her. She needed time to compose her emotions and sort out the ones she wanted to keep from the ones she had to bury. She chose to dispose of most of them.

He held the horse while she pulled herself into the saddle then swung up on his own mount. All he said was, "Let's go," in a voice that was an echo of the fading thunder.

They were riding again, faster, without stopping to check the trail. Brewster had mumbled something about knowing where to look. His eyes continually swept over their path, forever vigilant, lest he miss something.

The hills grew steeper, the trees thicker, the deciduous giving way to pine and spruce.

The sun regained its warmth and then lost it in the slanting evening rays.

Just when she wondered if they were going to ride forever, Brewster pulled up and waited for her to stop at his side. "We'll have to go much slower now." She turned to him, watching his eyes. In their depths was a warning—and something else. Something she shied away from. "The terrain is rough here—dangerous for both man and horse." The roll of grassy hills had given way to clumps of dirt, washouts, and scrubby trees fighting for survival. Abby shivered as she viewed the scene.

Dangerous! The word whirled through her brain. Was this what he had been worried about? She took a slow, steadying breath in a futile attempt to calm the riot of emotions. Her mind was as confused and tangled as the treacherous landscape they faced.

Brewster urged his horse forward through the dwarfed trees and broken branches.

"Wait," she begged, staring straight ahead, not seeing him or the rugged landscape. She was listening to the sounds inside her head. It was Andrew. She felt him.

"He's here," she nodded with utmost certainty.

"Where?" He looked at the maze of dips and hillocks.

"I don't know. But he is. I can feel him."

She met his eyes, daring him to disagree, but he simply lifted one eyebrow and said, "Then we better find him."

Find him. Two little words. It sounded so simple. Abby stared at the maze around her. There were gullies, some higher than a man's head, and mounds of earth like abandoned giant anthills. Her insides were so tight she could feel her heart thudding against her ribs and the blood gushing through her veins.

Find him! The words shrieked inside her head.

"Andrew!" She called over and over until her voice was hoarse. She knew he was there. Yet after several minutes they had found nothing to give them any assurance.

Brewster was looking to her right, guiding his horse over the clumps and around potholes.

"Andrew!" It was a wail. She nudged her horse forward, skirting a trench that angled westward, twisting and deepening as it went. The stunted trees reached out long, bony arms and dark, gnarled fingers, clutching at the light that was speeding away. Abby wanted to grab the sinking sun and force it to wait—to let them find Andrew before darkness descended. She knew this terrain would force them to call a halt to the search once the light faded. It wasn't worth a man's life, and that of his horse, to try to cross this at night. Her pulse pounded in the pit of her stomach. She tried to avoid thinking about Andrew. If he had ridden unaware into this insane scene, he might be—

She stopped her thoughts, but she couldn't prevent the pictures that flashed through her mind, of Andrew lying twisted and bent, his body broken on rocks and whitened stumps.

"Andrew!" she shrieked his name to the sky. And from the sky heard nothing but the mocking of three crows she had frightened from their evening routine.

God, she pleaded. *Where is he? Show us where to look. Please, please, please keep him—alive,* her mind screamed. *Oh, God, please,* she begged.

She let her horse munch a mouthful of grass and closed her eyes, waiting for peace to replace her panicked fears.

"Abigail, over here." Brewster waved at her. She gripped

the reins and kicked her heels.

"Be careful."

She nodded and watched the ground, knowing it would take the concentration of both her and her mount to avoid every hole and pile of tangled branches. In the wan light, it was hard to pick out a safe route until it was almost too late. She bit the inside of her lip. Her arms felt ready to snap. She didn't dare think about why Brewster had called her. He watched her until she had gone ten feet, then he dismounted and disappeared into a gully.

"Wait," she cried, but only the wind answered. She pressed the horse forward. Fifty yards from where Brewster's horse waited, she slid from the saddle and dashed toward the spot she had last seen him.

"Brewster, have you found him? Where are you?" She stumbled, her feet caught in a snarl of branches. Kicking herself free she didn't bother to stand up but ran with her hands almost touching the ground. Her skirt caught on a bush and she wrenched it free, clutching it in a crumpled ball. "Andrew," she whimpered his name as she scurried forward.

"Abigail, over here." Brewster's head appeared over the edge. She was almost there. She didn't slow her scuttling gait. Brewster grabbed her arm as she dived over the edge.

"Slow down," he rumbled.

"Did you find him? Where is he? Is he okay?" Her words tumbled out as tangled as the branches at her feet.

Grabbing her by the shoulders, Brewster forced her to stop and face him. His eyes shadowed by the lowering sun were impossible to read, but she saw the tense set of his jaw and stiffened. Her heartbeats filled her like the roar of rushing waters.

"I've found him," Brewster said, his face so close she could feel his breath fanning her cheek.

"Is he. . .?" She gulped.

"He's alive."

"Where is he? Let me go." She struggled to free herself,

but his hands dropped to her upper arms and he held her so tightly she couldn't shake free.

"Wait a minute. Listen to me." He held her until she met his eyes. Even in the half-light, she could feel them boring into hers. "He's alive, but his leg is broken."

"How bad?" She lost her voice and could barely get out a whisper.

"Bad."

Again she struggled.

"Hold on." He refused to release her. "He's in pain. But we're going to have to move him."

Her thudding heartbeat pooled in a heavy puddle deep in her gut.

He nodded as he saw she understood. "There isn't any way to do it without making his pain worse."

She moaned.

"Get yourself together. You've got to be strong now."

Forcing air into her lungs, sucking it down to the quivering pool inside, she drew strength from some place outside herself. A shudder raced up her spine and she nodded.

Still holding her shoulder, he guided her down the bank, steadying her when her foot skidded on loose gravel that scattered before her like dreams exploded by the sound of an alarm clock. Maybe it was all a dream. If so, she wished the alarm would sound now before she had to face Andrew, injured and in pain.

But no alarm sounded. Instead, Brewster's arm tightened around her shoulders and she knew the next step would take her around the corner of this narrow wash. She clamped her jaw so tight her teeth squeaked.

nine

All she could see was a shadowy form. With a cry, she broke from Brewster's grasp and hurried to Andrew's side, dropping to her knees.

He turned to her. "Abby." She had to bend to catch his words. "I knew you would come." His breath smelled like old socks and she pressed her hand to her mouth, then leaned closer, trying to make out every detail in the dusk.

Bruises on his face. Oh, his face!

Andrew's eyes were dull and sunken in gray cheeks. Her gaze raced across his body. A deep gash on his forearm. His pant leg—dark with blood—was torn back to reveal a swollen thigh. Even in this light, she could see the dull red of a massive bruise.

"Water," he mumbled.

The canteen lay at his side, just out of reach, but she could see the cap was off. How long had he been without water?

Behind her she heard Brewster leading the horses over the rocks, gravel clattering ahead of them, and then he pressed a full canteen into her hand. "Just a few swallows to start with," Brewster warned.

Andrew's breathing came in gasps and she hovered over him, wondering where she could touch him without increasing his pain. He lifted his left arm and grabbed for the water. She guided the jug to his mouth. His icy palm against her flesh felt like sandpaper, and she knew there were small stones imbedded in his hand.

Taking the canteen away, she capped it and set it aside.

"Andrew." It was a prayer, a plea. She wanted to touch every part of him to assure herself he was all right, but she was afraid of hurting him. She brushed back his hair, feeling

103

bits of dirt. "I'm so glad we found you. I was so worried." With shaking hands, she trailed her fingers down his cheeks. He winced as she touched a bruise and she pulled back but not before she realized that he was as cold as winter snow. He needed to get out of his wet clothes as soon as possible.

Again he grasped her hand. She took his hand between hers. "How long you been here?" she asked.

"I think this is the third day." His voice was reedy. "My horse tumbled into this drop-off and threw me."

She squeezed his hand but there was no need for more words. They said all they needed to through their hands.

Firelight flared, driving away the shadows. Brewster brushed his hands off and stood over them. She met his eyes for but a heartbeat then turned to study Andrew's leg. In the better light, she could see it bent unnaturally, and the smell of old blood oozed from a gash close to the knee.

She lifted her eyes to Brewster. She knew her expression must be bleak. It seemed they had found Andrew only to be powerless to help him. How were they going to deal with all his needs, especially out here? They had only a few cups of water. There were no supplies for cleansing the wound. He needed warm, dry clothes. Brewster's steady gaze remained on her. Finally he spoke. "We'll need some sort of bandages."

She nodded, glad to be able to do something, and turning her back to him, slipped her petticoat off and began to tear it into strips. The second petticoat to be ripped to shreds, she remembered.

He strode out of the light and was gone for several minutes before returning with several long, straight branches in his arms. Where had he found them? She remembered only bent and tangled wood around them.

He dropped close to the fire and knelt beside Abby. "Andrew." His voice had a ring to it she hadn't heard before. "We're going to have to set that leg before we can move you."

Andrew groaned softly and nodded.

"I expect it's going to hurt some."

Abby was surprised to see something flicker in Andrew's eyes and she darted a glance at Brewster in time to catch a blaze in his expression. A message had passed between the two men that she didn't understand. Grateful as she was for Brewster's help, she didn't like the silent contact Andrew had shared with him.

How petty, she scolded herself. It was just her reaction to seeing Andrew hurt that made her resentful, she rationalized.

Brewster pulled two of the longer sticks closer, arranging them in neat lines, then tied one of the blankets from the saddle roll across, fashioning a travois. Abby shuddered at the thought of Andrew bouncing across the rugged terrain in this shabby affair. When he was done, Brewster pulled out his knife.

"I'll have to cut his pants."

Before she could answer, he deftly sliced the pant leg from toe to hip, exposing the swollen flesh even more.

In unison, Abby and Andrew groaned.

"You want something to bite on while I do this?" he asked Andrew, offering him a green stick. When Andrew opened his mouth, he placed the stick between his teeth. Turning, Brewster looked at Abby. She read the question in his eyes.

"I'll be fine," she muttered, ignoring the way her stomach rolled.

"Hold his hands," Brewster ordered and she moved to do so while he moved toward Andrew's feet. Placing his legs on either side of Andrew, he grasped the foot. "Now," he barked and heaved on the injured leg.

Andrew moaned low in his throat, the sound ripping through Abby, tearing her in strips like she'd torn her petticoat. Then his head lolled to one side.

"He's passed out," Brewster grunted. "It's for the best. He won't feel anything for a few minutes." Already Brewster was placing the shorter branches on either side of Andrew's leg. "Help me bind it."

Her head spun, but she forced her fingers to obey, gathering up the strips of cloth. With steady hands, Brewster lifted

Andrew's leg so she could wrap it in the splints.

"Tighter," he ordered when her shaky hands let the bandage grow loose.

He held the leg with one hand and helped her wind the cloth, taking the roll from her hand and carrying it under Andrew's leg. Once, Andrew moaned and she dropped the strip.

"Keep going," he growled. Tears stung her eyes and she obeyed blindly, hating him for his lack of feeling.

As soon as they were finished, he lowered the leg carefully and pulled the travois closer. "I'll roll him toward me and you shove this under as far as you can."

"I can't," she whispered. "It will hurt him too much." She shook her head, looking everywhere but at him.

He reached across Andrew and grasped her chin, forcing her to meet his eyes. "He's out," he growled. "He can't feel a thing. Let's get it done before he comes to."

She swallowed hard. Her mouth felt like she'd rinsed it with ashes.

He waited.

She blinked. He braced himself on his knees and eased Andrew to his side. Abby shoved the rough contraption awkwardly under Andrew's back. With infinite care, Brewster eased him down then slipped the travois under him. Andrew remained unconscious.

"Well, let's go for those wet clothes while we have a chance. Get all the blankets from the bedrolls."

She scurried to obey. When she returned, Brewster had slit Andrew's clothes and eased them off, tossing them behind him. Together they tucked blankets around him as tightly as possible, but Abby knew it would do little to ease the jostling when they moved him.

Andrew moaned, his eyes open, pupils wide with pain.

"All done," she whispered.

Brewster hunkered down beside them. "We have to get you out of here," he addressed Andrew. "There's another storm coming up."

Abby heard thunder in the distance. "Where will we take him?" She half rose, pressing her hand to her mouth. It was miles back to their place. She knew Andrew would never make it.

"I know a place."

She stared at him, remembering the miner's dugout they had shared. *I sure hope it's better than that,* she thought.

Brewster turned away, unaware of her concerns, and murmuring instructions to his horse, he positioned the animal in front of the travois. He uncoiled his lariat, slipped loops over the ends of the branches and hooked it to his saddle. Slowly, he tightened the rope until Andrew's head was halfway up the horse's tail.

For a minute he studied Andrew. "That was the easy part, I'm afraid." He brought Abby's horse to her.

Her mouth felt slack jawed. For a moment she didn't move. It had to be the light, she decided, that made her think she had seen Brewster squeeze Andrew's shoulder in sympathy even as he shoved the reins toward her.

"I think I'll walk behind with Andrew," she murmured.

He nodded and led her horse as he mounted his own.

There was no way any of them could ease the roughness of the ride. Andrew grasped the sides of his conveyance until his knuckles shone white in the dying firelight. He clenched his jaw so tightly she could see the muscles below his ears quiver.

The firelight was far behind them, no longer giving the faintest illumination to the path. She stumbled on the uneven ground and barely stopped herself from grabbing the travois for support. Her rib cage squeezed painfully at the thought of how much pain it would give Andrew.

"Brewster, I'm ready to ride."

As she sank into the saddle, it finally hit her.

Andrew was hurt. Badly. She couldn't guess how badly but two nights in the open had made his condition worse.

She couldn't stop shaking. Brewster's low voice reached out to her in the darkness.

"He'll be fine. Hang in there."

Now why did he go and do that? She was doing just fine, but his unexpected kindness jarred the tears from her and she scrubbed at her eyes.

Either the man has eyes like an owl, or he's memorized every inch of this country, she thought, as they plodded one weary mile after another.

Tiredness was long past—something she felt hours ago when her legs quivered and her back screamed for rest. Now she was beyond feeling. All her energies were concentrated on staying upright in the saddle. It was impossible to keep both eyes open at the same time. Her chin kept falling to her chest despite her attempts to keep upright. She felt herself tipping and snapped her head upright, forcing both eyes wide open, but she was powerless to keep them open.

"Abigail, we're here."

At his low voice, she lifted her head. When had they stopped moving? Or had they? Her muscles vibrated with movement but she couldn't hear hoofbeats. In the silvery starlight, she saw Brewster standing at her side.

"You can get down."

"Umm," she sighed, trying to nod her head. But her chin settled into the collar of her coat.

"Abigail. Wake up."

I am awake, she thought, but it took too much energy to say the words.

"Come on. Get down."

She kicked her feet from the stirrups and lifted herself from the saddle. At least she thought she did, yet her hand still clasped the saddle horn. Again she ordered her muscles to complete the task, but they were as responsive as sticks of wood. She felt like a stuffed gunnysack.

"Here we go."

Strong arms grabbed her waist and lifted her from the saddle. She felt so heavy, like a water-soaked log, yet she was floating.

"Hang on there."

The words drifted above her head. Warm breath caressed her face. She snuggled against a comforting chest.

"Umm," she sighed and nestled into the protection of a strong pair of arms.

⁂

Sunlight turned her eyelids into a scarlet screen and warmed her cheek, but Abby kept her eyes closed, letting awareness seep in with the scent of pine needles. The first thing that registered was that her whole body ached like it had been through a butter churn. And she had her clothes on, except for her shoes. She reached out her hands and knew instantly it was not her bed.

Then she remembered the long ride and being carried. Her cheeks warmed as she recalled how she'd nuzzled into his embrace like an adoring bride.

She bolted upright and flung the covers back. Flinging open the door of the bedroom, she dashed into the next room and skidded to a halt. Andrew lay on a sofa, his leg cradled on either side by a rolled blanket. She stared down at him. His cheeks were pale in contrast to the purple bruises on them. He slept with his lips parted. Occasionally, he moved and groaned. Tears stung her eyes. She wanted to touch him; assure herself he was really there.

His eyelids fluttered and slowly opened. He stared at nothing then gradually focused on her.

"Hi." He sounded like a frog with a cold.

Her legs turned to cotton and she dropped to the edge of the sofa and touched his cheek. "Hi." She smiled weakly.

"I never got a chance to ask you last night. Are you all right?" He searched her face.

She nodded. "You want some water?" She looked around. There was a cup of water on the table next to the couch. She picked it up and glanced around the room. The kitchen and eating area at the far end were as efficient and clean as a dream. A large cast-iron sink in a row of neat cupboards boasted its own pump. The table was round oak. She thought of how plain their hand-hewn plank table looked in comparison.

Though dusty, the wood floor held a gleam of beauty. She checked over her shoulder and saw a huge fieldrock fireplace that took up the entire wall behind them. The whole room was beautiful. It glowed with warmth and she decided it was because of the books. The entire lower half of the room was bookcases filled with books. Two huge paintings hung on the inside wall. One showed a cabin nestled in foothills surrounded by towering mountains. It washed her with a sense of peace. The other picture was a riot of blue flowers parting for a narrow path leading to a wicker settee on which lay a white straw bonnet and an open book as if waiting for someone to return. A surge of joy swept over her at the scene.

There was a thin layer of dust everywhere, suggesting the owners might be too busy to tend to household chores, but whoever built this house and lived in it must be deeply sensitive and refined. She longed to meet them.

"Who owns this place?" she whispered to Andrew as she handed him the glass of water.

Andrew slanted his eyes to a spot past her shoulder. She turned and for the first time saw Brewster stretched out asleep in front of the fireplace.

"Him?"

"Yes."

"You sure?" They were whispering.

"He told me last night."

The travois lay bundled on the floor. "How did he get you in here?"

"He pulled me in on that thing."

"By himself?" She tried to imagine Brewster dragging Andrew into the house and across the room. She remembered how easily he had thrown her onto his horse, but Andrew weighed close to two hundred pounds.

"I helped some getting on the couch."

"Ow. That must have hurt."

"I think I was past caring. Anything that didn't move or bump sounded pretty inviting even if I had to drag my leg to get there."

"I should have helped."

"Yes, you should have, but you were out like a light. Anyway, he was most kind about it. Who is he? He told me his name is Brewster Johnson, but where did he come from?"

"He's the man who. . ." She hesitated, not wanting to upset Andrew.

"I'm the man who kidnapped her." Brewster's deep voice finished her sentence.

Abby stiffened, her cheeks burning at the memory of last night. She prayed he wasn't looking at her. She held her breath, waiting for Andrew's reaction.

"So that's what happened to you. I wondered, and imagined all sorts of things." He held her gaze, searching her eyes for satisfaction. "Did he hurt you?"

She shook her head, but it was Brewster who answered.

"I did not. And I brought her back home."

Andrew's lips twitched. "I always knew it would be hard to find a man who would keep you." His eyes closed and she saw how drawn his face was.

"You rest now." She patted his shoulder and hovered over him, reluctant to face the other man at her side.

"I'd better check that leg," Brewster muttered.

She stepped aside, grateful that he kept his back to her. She forgot everything as she watched him lift the strips of cloth and look at the swollen leg. Straightening himself, he stood looking down at Andrew. She waited, shuffling as the minute lengthened into two.

"What is it?"

He shook his head. "Let him rest for now. I think we could all use a decent meal."

She followed him to the kitchen, aware he had not answered her question. Glancing over her shoulder at Andrew, already sleeping, she wondered what had grabbed Brewster's attention, but he refused to meet her eyes and she knew he would not tell her until he was ready.

Andrew woke long enough to take a few spoonfuls of thin oatmeal and another draught of water, then he waved her away and fell back to sleep.

Brewster left the house as soon as he had eaten his breakfast, but later, as Abby sat watching Andrew, he returned. She met his eyes, trying to find clues about this man who helped a stranger, gave efficient medical help, constructed a home that was much more than a simple cabin, and yet kidnapped a woman for his wife. His hazel eyes darkened as she searched their depths, but his secrets remained hidden. He would reveal nothing.

"Did he eat something?" He dropped his eyelids and looked at Andrew.

"A little. Is he going to be all right?"

He kept his eyes lowered as her heart leapt with fear. Then his eyes, narrowed and hardened, met hers. "I don't know. There was a hand on one of the outfits I worked who had a break like this. He. . ." He shrugged and didn't finish.

Abby's heart turned to stone and she stared openmouthed at him.

"Course every day he got bounced about in the wagon. Don't suppose that did him much good."

She didn't move or blink.

He flung his hat to the floor and strode to her side. "Abigail, snap out of it. He'll likely recover in fine form if he gets proper nursing and that's up to you." He drew her toward the stove. "There's lots of firewood and all you have to do for water is pump the handle. Now heat up some water and make some compresses." He opened a cupboard and handed her a small tin. "Add Epsom salts to the water. Keep hot compresses on that swollen area above his knee." Returning to the door, he scooped his hat off the floor and watched her. "I'll be gone a day or so. Two at the most." He jammed on his hat and left.

ten

The next morning, as Abby waited for the water to boil, she watched as a milky curtain of fog lifted from the valley and honey sunshine poured over the treetops, dipped under the eaves, and flooded the house with warm light.

You wouldn't call this place a cabin, she thought. It was really and truly a house—a warm, inviting home. When he said he had a house of sorts, she had imagined a mean, narrow cabin with a slit of a window and a dirt floor. Not these rich, hand-rubbed planks.

The pot bubbled and she stirred in the salts, one tablespoon at a time, until it grew murky. Plunging in a clean cloth, she scooped it out with a wooden spoon, laying it in a basin until it was cool enough for her to gingerly pick up two corners and fold it into a neat square. Flipping it from hand to hand, she hurried to Andrew's side. He watched her warily, knowing she would only let it cool enough to prevent a burn before she placed it on his red and swollen leg. His jaw tightened and he clenched his fists.

Patting the cloth, she decided it had cooled enough, and avoiding his eyes, laid it on the wound with infinite care. He stiffened and moaned. The sound dropped into her stomach like she had swallowed a rock.

"Is it getting worse?" she asked.

His eyes were clouded and he didn't answer right away. When he did, his voice was thin, threading its way into the depths of her brain. "It's hard to say."

His pain stung her like a dip in boiling water. "If only I could do something. Give you something." Her inadequacy burned.

"You're here." The stabbing pain settled. He unclenched

113

his fists and his eyes focused. "Tell me what happened."

She searched for the end of a thread that went somewhere. "He wanted a wife," she began, plucking at the first loose end. She told him about Sam and Petey and how Brewster had exploded with anger. For the first time, it dawned on her that he might have been killed. She shuddered as she thought what that would have meant to her personal safety.

Bit by bit, she unraveled her story. When she had finished, Andrew, whose eyes had remained fixed on her, said, "Wow. Sounds like something from a book." His hand touched hers. "I'm just glad you're safe and sound."

She nodded, echoing his words in her mind.

"Abby? Did you pray?"

"Like never before in my life."

"Me too. And even harder when I broke my leg and my horse ran off and I was stranded in the middle of nowhere."

"And our prayers were answered."

He nodded and she knew his thoughts matched hers. It was the first time they had realized how much they needed God's intervention. And He had proven faithful. She squeezed his hand.

"I'm scared," she whispered. "We're all alone here and your leg looks bad." She shivered in spite of her attempt to remain strong. She should have remembered she couldn't hide the truth from Andrew.

He nodded and said, "Let's pray together."

She nodded and bowed her head until it almost touched Andrew's forehead. They took turns praying for safety and healing for Andrew's leg. Andrew thanked God for the fact they were both safe.

When they were done, Abby felt her tension ease away.

"One thing I don't understand. Why kidnap a wife? Why not court a woman? Or simply ask her right out?"

She shrugged. "Maybe it took too much effort." The words he had said that first day came to her mind. "Besides, he thinks he's ugly." More things came to her now—the bitterness in his voice when he spoke of Lucy, his avowal that he didn't believe in anything. "Probably most of all because he doesn't trust anyone. This way, he doesn't expect anything so he can't be hurt if he never gets it."

"Strange man, yet he seems so straight." Andrew's eyes drooped.

"Yes," she agreed. She pulled the thick, gray blanket to his chin and slipped away.

Yes, strange, she thought as she circled the room. The collection of books surprised her, but not as much as her discovery that the wide windows gleamed like freshly washed china. Why would he keep his windows so clean despite his confessed lack of time for household chores? And there were so many windows.

The room grew warm. She opened the door and stood gazing out. Birds peppered the sky above the trees, their wings sifting the air. Insects hummed and chattered.

She picked up a corner of the cloth compress, careful not to waken Andrew. Several hours later, the skin of his leg glistened like a polished apple, but she couldn't tell if there was any improvement. Andrew continued to sleep, giving her plenty of time to think.

She recalled how she had one day watched a ropemaker at work, twisting long strands until they were taut, then joining the twisted strands to make a rope. She felt like one of those strands—and the crank was still turning.

Suddenly one of the strands broke and whirled out of control. How dare Brewster ride away, oblivious to Andrew's pain and her worry. He'd left her with no way of getting help. She didn't even know where she was.

Pressing back the burning in her chest, she continued applying compresses to Andrew's leg, praying it was enough. There was little else she could do.

The afternoon shadows were growing long when rocks clattered outside and a knock sounded.

Before she could call out, the door flew open and a

dark-suited man stepped in.

"I'm Dr. Baker." He smiled without changing the expression on his round face. "Where's the patient?" He saw Andrew and without waiting for a reply, stepped to his side. "I presume this is where I'm needed."

Abby shook aside her surprise. "Thank you for coming, but how did you know?"

"Mr. Johnson informed me. Fact of the matter is, he rode out with me." As he talked, he pulled aside the compress and probed the reddened area. Andrew flinched. Abby stepped toward the doctor then halted as he grunted and pulled aside the blanket. His hands felt along Andrew's collarbone, and down each arm, pausing as Andrew flinched again. He turned Andrew's arm over and examined an ink-colored bruise. As his hands moved, his mouth kept pace.

"Quite the hero, your Mr. Johnson."

Abby met Andrew's eyes and read the warning in them. She pressed back her accusations about Brewster.

"Single-handed he brought in two ruffians who have been terrorizing the country."

Abby and Andrew asked each other the same silent question. Was it Sam and Petey?

"Seems they've been responsible for robbing the stagecoach, helping themselves to a few cattle and stealing from some of the ranch houses. I heard tell one of Coyote John's daughters was raped. 'Spect these fellows are responsible." He pulled some bottles from his bag. "Dissolve this in water and use it for compresses. It will work a little better. Something I mixed up myself." He dropped several small packets into her palm. "Give him this for relief of his pain." He gave her instructions, jabbing his finger at her as he talked as if he were drilling the words into her.

"Yes, sir," he continued, closing his bag. "Must have been quite a thing for that young man to bring those two in by himself. I wish I could have seen it. Fact is, he probably could have sold seats to the event. They were hopping mad. Kept saying as how they would get even. But I don't expect they'll be much threat. They'll soon be wearing neckties so tight it'll give them a permanent headache."

The door squeaked open and Brewster faced them, a carpet-bag in his hand that she recognized from Andrew's room.

He's brought us clothes! she thought, her cheeks warming as she pictured him entering her room. Yet she had to admit she would be glad for a fresh outfit.

"Why, here's your young man now."

He's not my young man, she wanted to scream, but Dr. Baker was headed for the door. "Wait, Doctor. How is he? Is his leg going to be all right?"

He paused and turned to face her. "Looks pretty fair. Pretty fair. Couldn't have set it better myself. Just keep him still. I don't want him moved for six weeks. I'll check on him in a few days."

He passed Brewster in the doorway and squeezed his shoulder. "Good work there, son."

And he was gone as quickly as he had come. If she didn't hold the paper packages and bottle of salts in her hands she would have thought he was a mirage. Andrew must have had the same feeling for he let his breath out in a whoosh. "Bit like a cyclone, isn't he?"

Brewster closed the door and moved toward the cold fireplace, but no one answered Andrew's question.

"Brewster." At Andrew's call, he turned and faced him. "Was it Sam and Petey?"

He nodded.

Andrew spoke first. "How did you manage to apprehend them so quickly?"

Brewster shrugged. "Didn't take much. I figgered they'd be on my trail so I circled around them and waited where I knew I could get the drop on them."

No one spoke and the silence deepened around them.

"I guess that leaves you. What shall I do about you?" At Andrew's question, Abby looked directly at Brewster. He studied the floor at his feet. Finally, he cleared his throat and lifted his head to meet Andrew's eyes.

"I think that is up to you."

Her breathing was loud. Neither man looked away, and again she felt alone as she watched them measure each other and come to a conclusion that excluded her.

Andrew broke the silence. "All's well that ends well." Knowing he'd made up his mind, Abby turned away, tears stinging her eyes. *What about what he did to me?* she wanted to scream. *He kidnapped me and dragged me back and forth across the country.*

Yes, a little voice argued, *and he took you home. And then helped you find Andrew.* She clenched her fists at her side, drowning in a flood of emotion.

"You'll stay here as long as you need," Brewster said.

Andrew nodded. "Appreciate that."

So all the questions were answered, Abby fumed. But no one had taken into consideration her feelings or asked her what she wanted. It was one of the rare times in her life that she was truly angry at her twin.

"I need some fresh air," she muttered and marched out, controlling the urge to slam the door. *As if they'd notice,* she raged, feeling as forgotten as yesterday's sunrise.

She hurried down the path, giving no thought to where she went. *How could Andrew so easily ignore the fact that Brewster kidnapped me?* she thought. Did he not think how frightening it had been? And to dismiss it so simply with "all's well that ends well." As if the path taken to arrive at their destination was of no concern. Truth was, she decided, her ordeal meant nothing to anyone but herself. Andrew and Brewster had come to some sort of conclusion without speaking a word.

She stomped her foot on the damp grass. How dare Brewster think he could get away with this? He should have to pay. Like Sam and Petey. Brewster should have turned himself in at the same time.

Yes, and then where would you be? a little voice nagged. *Stuck out here with an injured brother. How would you cope?*

I'd find a way, she fumed. *Without his help. And how could Andrew agree to staying here after what Brewster has done?*

What has he done? the annoying voice argued. *Rescued both of you, gone for help, seen that your pursuers were in jail.*

As if that cancels out what he did, she argued with the persistent voice.

Maybe you should think of Andrew. He can't be moved if you want his leg to heal properly, the voice insisted.

Fine, she grunted. *I'll stay for Andrew. Just until he can travel. Not one minute more. But I won't change my mind about Brewster. He deserves to be punished.*

For a long time she stood looking over the valley, refusing to allow the beauty of the evening to soothe her. The shadows turned as purple as the folds in a velvet cape and the trees whispered secrets.

God loves him. The statement echoed inside her head.

She'd already tried to tell him that.

What had he said about a dump? God was a garbage dump for unloved people. Did she agree? Of course not. It's just that—that—

She crossed her arms and squared her jaw. She didn't want to think about it. She knew God loved her and had answered her prayers to find Andrew. If God wanted to love Brewster too, that was fine with her. But it didn't change anything.

She yawned, suddenly very tired. It had been a long, tension-wrapped day on the heels of many such days and nights. She turned toward the house.

It took longer than she expected to retrace her steps. By the time she returned, she was too tired to fight. She would, she concluded, be polite, even if he didn't deserve it.

&

It was the smell of coffee that tugged Abby from her sleep the next morning. She sprang from the bed and into her clothes and bolted to the door, where she skidded to a stop. Brewster had pulled a chair to the side of the sofa and he and Andrew were chatting away like old friends, each enjoying a steaming cup of coffee. It had always been her job to make Andrew his morning coffee and she wanted to fling away the cups and pour out the pot on the stove.

"Good morning," Andrew said.

Brewster rose so quickly the chair skidded away. He let his eyes rest on her for a fleeting moment then strode toward the stove. She could hear the humming fire and the purring kettle. The firebox was full of wood. At home, she usually got her own wood. Annoyance made her tighten her lips. A flash of color caught her eye and she stared at the jar of flowers in the center of the table. Red fireweed, orange paintbrush, blue-bells, yellow brown-eyed Susans sang a cheery greeting as gentle perfume bathed the air. Flowers, of all things. Didn't the man have anything better to do with his time? Her gaze lingered another heartbeat, then she turned to Andrew.

"Good morning and how are you feeling today?"

"Much better. Thanks to those powders the doctor left." The lines in his face had disappeared but his voice was deep, his eyelids heavy with the effect of the painkiller. Brewster must have given him some earlier.

I would have come if Andrew called, she fumed. It was her job.

Ignoring Brewster, who sprang out of the way at her approach, she hurried to make porridge, sitting at Andrew's side to eat her own breakfast when it was ready. As soon as Brewster wolfed down his food, he grabbed his hat and the rifle from over the door and left. Abby kept her face turned toward the floor. Not even to herself would she admit the tiny pang of loss as the door closed behind him.

It took only a few minutes to clean the kitchen and look after the compresses on Andrew's leg before he fell asleep. Circling the room, wondering what to do with the long hours stretching before her, Abby began to pull books from the shelves. Her wonder grew as she examined them. *He must own every book ever published,* she decided. She spent a long time paging through a set of wonderfully illustrated bird books. Flipping open the pages of *The Last Of The Mohicans,* by James Fenimore Cooper, she was soon lost in a world of Indians, settlers, and the wilds of the Americas. A banging noise caused her to clutch at her throat. Had she raced into a trap? Her eyes focused and she mentally returned to the house in which she sat, staring openmouthed and wide-eyed at Brewster.

"I brought you some meat for supper." His voice was rough and low as he held up two small birds, already plucked and cleaned, then dropped them into the basin. Without another word and before she could find her voice, he closed the door behind him. She could hear his boots thump down the path. In a few minutes, she heard hammering from across the clearing.

She covered the birds with water and set a pot of soup to simmer, then returned to her reading, where she stayed until it was time to serve the soup.

Brewster came slowly through the door. Abby turned her back, busying herself at the stove. She didn't look at him until she set the bowl of soup before him, but he kept his head down so she couldn't see his face. *That's fine with me,* she thought. She didn't want to see his eyes and the wariness in them at her continued coldness. She steeled herself to remain angry.

After she cleaned the kitchen, she changed Andrew's compresses and made sure he was comfortable before she again picked up her book from the shelf. Much later, with reluctance, she set it aside as the afternoon heat crowded in on her, but she knew she must put the birds in the oven if supper was to be ready on time. Despite the allure of the fictional world, she would not allow Brewster an opportunity to think her lazy.

Andrew wakened off and on through the day but seemed disinclined to talk. Knowing sleep would hasten his healing, she left him.

Late in the afternoon, he awoke, his eyes alert as he watched her every move. Something about the way he watched her made her uneasy, but he shook his head when she asked him what it was.

After they had eaten the evening meal in near silence, Brewster left the room with a mumbled explanation about having to check on the horses.

"Abby," Andrew called as the door closed. "Come here."

Drying her hands on a white linen towel, she hurried to his side.

"I've been watching you."

She nodded.

"And something's been bothering me."

Again she nodded as a lump swelled in the back of her throat.

"You've never been an unfriendly person, yet when Brewster's around, you are. What's the problem?"

"I'm not." She protested, knowing it was futile to argue with her twin. She was only surprised he seemed so thick about why. "All right, I suppose I am. But who could blame me? He kidnapped me. And it doesn't seem like anybody cares."

He opened his mouth but before he could speak, she hurried on. "And it's his fault you're lying here injured. Is it any wonder I don't feel like being friendly?"

"But Abby, I've never known you to be unforgiving." His voice was low, but his words stung like he'd flung acid in her face. "He made a mistake and he knows it and is trying his best to make it right. What more can you ask?"

What more? she asked herself. *Revenge. Justice. Not to see you and him visiting like old buddies.*

When she didn't answer, Andrew went on. "He seems so lonely. And so wary." He shook his head. "That doesn't seem fair. This is his house and he's going out of his way to look after us. Can't you try a little harder?"

Her best friend, protector, and defender had become her

accuser. She closed her eyes until she could swallow the sting of tears. Was she being petty and unforgiving? Andrew seemed to think so. She couldn't bear to have his disapproval.

Opening her eyes, she whispered, "I'll try."

"Good." He squeezed her hand as the door opened. He held it firmly, expectantly, as Brewster entered the room.

"I want to thank you for your hospitality and kindness," she blurted before she could change her mind, feeling her cheeks warm as she spoke.

Brewster halted midstep and raised his eyes to hers, holding her gaze for a long, tense moment. His expression became guarded and wary.

"You're welcome." His voice was a low rumble that rattled across her mind and tugged at her breastbone. The brittleness that had held her tight all day softened. Nothing had changed, she reasoned. Least of all, her feelings. She would always hate him. Perhaps hate was too strong a word. She would always dislike him, she amended, but being friendly? Andrew was right. It was the least she could do.

eleven

Abby gave Andrew the *Farmer's Almanac,* then curled up in the wine-colored armchair with her book. Brewster stared into the cold fireplace while the warm dusk settled around them, a welcome breeze stirring through the open windows, cloaking the room in the scent of wildflowers. Finally, with a deep sigh, Brewster grabbed a chair from next to the table, plunked it beside the bookcase, and lifted the lid of a gramophone. Abby had never seen a gramophone before, and over the top of her book she kept an eye on Brewster's movements. He put a cylinder on the sleeve, then wound a small, black handle before dropping the needle. At first, the music was too fast—thin and reedy—then it swelled into sweetness and filled the room. Abby closed her eyes and leaned back, letting the melody lift her and flood her chest with both sad and joyous emotions. The music died and she kept her eyes closed, lost in the swirl of emotions. Slowly, as if rising from a coma, she lifted her eyelids and saw Brewster tipped back in his chair, his head resting on the golden log wall, his eyes closed, his lashes like a dark fan against his cheeks. Surrounded by the effects of the music and the warm color of logs and book bindings, his face looked younger, softer, warmer. His eyelids drifted upward and he stared straight at her. The sweetness produced by the gramophone had stripped away his pretenses, broken down his guard, allowing her to see past his eyes into his soul. She saw his naked hunger, his stark longing for someone to care about the unloved boy-man inside. In an instant, his expression hardened and the shades were drawn as surely as if a hand had reached up and pulled the blinds. He dropped his chair to the floor with a thud.

"That was swell," Andrew sighed. "I've never heard anything like that. Do you have any more?"

"Some." Carefully, he removed the cylinder and placed on another, then cranked the handle again.

A rousing tune filled the room.

"Camptown races start tonight,

"Do dah, Do dah. . ."

By the end of the song Andrew was chuckling. "Could we hear it again?"

The second time around, Andrew joined in the chorus of "do dah, do dah" and the third time, raised his hands as though conducting a band. "Everyone sing," he urged.

By keeping her eyes fixed on her brother, Abby was able to forget Brewster's tight look as she sang along. Andrew asked for it again and sang the entire song, with Abby joining in on the do-dahs. She almost lost her voice when a third voice—deep and full—joined her partway through. She and Andrew smiled at each other, sharing a joint victory in knowing they had succeeded in getting Brewster to have a little fun. By the fourth time through, the twins were laughing and when Abby turned to include Brewster, she was surprised to see that he almost smiled. At least, she thought, if you could call a slight lifting of his mouth and a deepening of the creases at the corner of his eyes a smile. She had to admit she liked what it did to his features, gentling the hard planes and the slash across his cheek. But it was his eyes that trapped her. They were the color of pine needles and full of deep, dark mysteries.

It was absurd to think about such things, she scolded herself.

Andrew broke the silence. "You have so many books and all those phonographs. I don't think I've ever seen such a lot. Not even in the library back in the old country. It certainly didn't boast a gramophone."

Brewster rose from his chair. "They're my friends." He closed the lid and carefully replaced the cylinders.

"I'll get you settled for the night," Abby said to Andrew. A few minutes later, she was in the narrow bedroom with Brewster's words still ringing in her ears. As she brushed her hair, she felt moisture at the corner of her eyes and dashed it away with the back of her hand. It was due to the music and the scent of flowers and pine needles. It had nothing to do with Brewster's lonesome words now blaring through her head. She was getting far too emotional if his statements got under her skin that easily.

Over the past days she'd seen a glimpse of his unhappy childhood and how it had shaped him as a man who didn't trust relationships. Yet in this house she had a peek of something else. The music, the flowers, the books all pointed toward fine things. Things, she was sure, he'd deny and reject if she mentioned them.

Was it possible for him to learn to trust people? To love and be loved? Was that why he had kidnapped her? Had he thought he saw in her someone he could trust?

She clutched the hairbrush in both hands, staring out into the silent darkness. Her heart thrilled to think someone would see her in that light.

Then she flung the brush aside. *What difference does it make what he thinks?* she fumed. Despite his comments about needing help, he seemed to manage very well on his own. And with the books and gramophone to enrich his life, he had no need for friendship.

She knew her thoughts were unfair and likely untrue, but she clung to them as she climbed into bed and pulled the covers close. It suited her to think the way she did.

The next morning, she hurried from her room determined to be the first up. Andrew lay asleep on the sofa, his hair mussed and his covers tangled. She felt a pang as she realized he must have found it difficult to get comfortable. Brewster had moved to the smaller bedroom, leaving her the one he normally used. The door to his room remained closed. Moving as quietly as she could, Abby built the fire and put the coffee to boil. Within a few minutes, Andrew stirred and moaned. Abby hurried over to put on a fresh compress, ignoring Andrew's muttered complaints. He was always grumpy in the morning and she had learned long ago to pay little attention. She was hurrying back to the kitchen with her hands full when the bedroom door opened and Brewster appeared, his dark hair sleek as usual. Determined to establish a friendly atmosphere, she set two places on the table before taking Andrew a cup of coffee.

Filling both mugs on the table, she called, "Coffee's ready. Come and have some breakfast." She sat, her hands folded in her lap, and waited for Brewster to join her.

She prayed silently and began to eat.

Brewster's eyes darted from Andrew to Abby and then to the floor. He pulled out the chair across from her and lowered himself into it as if he expected the seat to drop out.

"Thank you for bringing in the flowers." She would make this a pleasant experience, she decided, even if she had to carry the conversation entirely on her own. If she had any power over the situation they would all act as if this were a normal everyday event.

"Welcome," he grunted, gulping a swallow of coffee.

She continued. "The mountain flowers seem so bold and showy."

Brewster darted a glance at the flowers. Before she could see what his expression said, he lowered his head and studied his plate.

"Don't you think so?" she persisted.

His fork hovered halfway to his mouth. "I guess so." He gobbled his food then pushed back his chair. "I best get to work."

"What are you doing? For work, I mean?"

He was poised on the edge of his chair, prepared for flight. "Making some fence."

Andrew perked up. "You running horses?"

"A few. Mostly cows. I bought some breeding stock from

the Bar U when I bought this place."

"Herefords?"

"Shorthorn." He edged toward the door, eyeing his hat.

"Well, have a good day," she called as he pulled open the door.

He jammed the hat on his head and fled.

"What was that all about?" Andrew demanded.

"What?"

"All that eye batting and moony looks. You scared the man half to death."

She drew herself up. "I did not. You said I should try to be friendly, so I was." She turned away, ignoring his snort.

The first morning set the tone for the following days. Abby set out to draw Brewster into conversation and when he responded even slightly, she almost cheered. At the same time, Brewster did all he could to ease life for her. Whether he did it intentionally or out of habit, she didn't know. He provided a supply of fresh meat. He kept the wood box full. One day he brought a pan of blackberries and set them on the table. She baked them in a pie. Andrew, whose appetite improved daily, ate two pieces and raved about the treat. Brewster said little but ate three pieces and thanked her hoarsely. Berries appeared every three or four days after that.

The doctor came and checked Andrew's leg, declaring it was healing nicely and said Abby could discontinue the compresses. They all sighed with relief, knowing it would now be possible to let the fire die down during the heat of the day. Dr. Baker also brought the news that Sam and Petey had been transported to Fort Calgary, tried and convicted, and were now rotting in the fort's jail. The country could breathe easier with those two gone, he drawled, and Abby couldn't help but agree. She knew she would breathe easier and slanted a glance at Brewster. His dark gaze met hers for a moment before he turned away to listen to the doctor.

The days folded into each other, warm and contented.

We're learning to be friends, she thought.

As soon as she got up, Abby knew the day was different. It started as she left her bedroom.

"About time you showed up," Andrew groused.

"It's barely light. You were expecting me in the middle of the night?" She bit her lip, wishing she had kept silent. She knew responding to Andrew's early morning moods only provoked him. And she was right.

"It's hours since it grew light and I've been lying here like a sack of potatoes. You know I can't do anything by myself. I'm beginning to think you're enjoying my helplessness." He glowered at her.

"Like I haven't looked after you every hour of every day for the last three weeks. Did you ever think I might want a break?"

"It's me that has the break, I might remind you."

"Like I need reminding," she growled.

A thud sounded on the closed bedroom door. "Quiet," a voice grated.

"Humph." She flung her head back and stomped to the kitchen, ignoring Andrew's steaming glare.

Outside, the clouds hung low and threatening, shutting out the morning sunshine. Without the bright morning light, the house seemed dull and lifeless.

Brewster joined them for breakfast, but after glancing at brother and sister and seeing their scowling expressions, he kept to himself.

I'm in such a bad mood, I think I'll bake cookies. Abby threw more wood on the fire and gathered up her supplies.

The clouds clung to the treetops like a tent to its pegs. By late afternoon, a fine mist began to descend. Brewster came in and shook the moisture from his hat.

"Looks like it's going to settle in for a good pour."

Great, thought Abby, and she turned to pull a sheet of cookies from the oven.

Andrew grunted.

"I'll build a fire in the fireplace. Help take the chill out of the air." In a few minutes, flames danced merrily at the far end of the room. Abby stared at them, feeling the depression lift from her shoulders.

After supper, Brewster pulled the sofa closer to the fire for Andrew, and Abby drew the armchair close. Brewster set his own chair a little way from the twins, but still drawn up to the fire. Abby set out a plate of cookies and a huge pot of tea.

"This is nice," Andrew said, his earlier peevishness forgotten.

I guess I can't blame him for feeling restless at times, Abby thought. *It's hard for him to have to lie there day after day. On the whole, he's been a good patient. Besides,* she concluded, *it's this rotten weather as much as anything that's making us cranky.*

"You know what it reminds me of?" Andrew turned to her, his eyes sparkling.

She shook her head.

"You remember that time when we were about, oh, I suppose six or seven, and Father was cleaning up the garden? It must have been late October. I remember the big pile of leaves, and cornstalks, and old grass. It was already dark when he lit the fire. Remember?"

She nodded as memories trailed across her mind, warm and cozy as a wool quilt. "I remember how warm it was. Like the night was just a silken curtain. And the flames were orange monsters that licked at the sky. We ran around and around the fire. Widening our circle until we hovered between light and dark."

"Daring the darkness to frighten us."

"Yes. Exactly. Begging to be scared."

"Remember what Papa did?" He had unconsciously shifted to his childhood name for their father.

"I remember." Her voice bubbled with laughter and joy. "It was one of the few times I remember him really playing with us. And laughing so much."

"There were still some cornstalks to be pulled. . ."

"And we would hide behind them as Papa yanked them out. . ."

"And he would. . ."

"Lunge. . ."

"And growl. . ."

"And pretend to scare us."

They tripped over each other as they told Brewster their story.

"Then we ran around the fire and he. . ."

"Would wait for us and grab us. . ."

"And throw us up in the air."

Abby and Andrew looked at each other and grinned. "I screamed with laughter until I felt weak," she said.

"Me, too."

"It was the best day of my life. I felt so safe and happy."

"Guess that's why I like a fire so much."

"Umm. Me, too."

She looked at Brewster. His eyes shifted from Andrew to her. Her heart leaped to her throat as she saw his unvarnished longing. Hunger. A dog too often kicked and now afraid to take the bone offered him by a kind stranger.

"How 'bout you, Brewster? You must have sat around many a fire. What memories come to mind when you see the flames?" Andrew asked.

Abby saw Brewster's face drain. His skin was gray and bleak as he stared into the fire without answering. The log cracked. A flame leaped up the chimney. Sparks sprayed against the screen. Rain pattered against the shingles. Still he did not answer. Lost in his own thoughts, Andrew seemed not to notice, but Abby's chest grew tighter and tighter until she was afraid she was going to choke.

Brewster sighed and Abby eased in a little air.

"I can't say I have any memories that make me feel safe and happy like you do." His voice was almost lost in the depths of his chest. "My earliest memories are of crouching in a corner, straining for the least little sound that would warn

me that Lucy was coming. But I did like to watch sunbeams."
His voice deepened. "I would find a spot where I could see
one. Didn't matter if it was coming through a crack between
the boards, or through a bit of glass, or even a door hanging
by one hinge. I liked to watch the shaft of light cross the floor
and crawl the walls, catching bits of dust that danced and
skipped in the light. Guess the firelight sort of reminds me of
that." He rubbed his cheek, drawing his finger along the scar
as if feeling some deep, driving pain. "Guess I was a bit of a
dreamer. No wonder Lucy was always getting mad at me."
He shook his shoulders. "I hunkered down around enough
campfires over the years trying to stay dry or find a way to
get both sides warm at once that I promised myself when I
had a place of my own, it would have a fireplace big enough
a body could hope to get himself warm clear through."

Andrew had never heard Brewster speak of Lucy and his
childhood and Abby could feel his shock. "Who was Lucy
and why were you crouching in corners?" His voice was
sharp with horror.

The hardness slipped back into place. Brewster's face
looked lean and so filled with pain that Abby bit her lip to
keep from crying out.

"Lucy was my mother and she didn't want anyone to know
I was there so I learned to hide and be quiet. I tried to become
invisible but I never quite figured out how." He gave a
twisted smile.

"Why?" Andrew whispered, his voice echoing Abby's
incredulity. Although she had heard some of it before, she
still shuddered at what he had suffered as a child.

Brewster shrugged, hard planes angling his face. "I guess a
kid wasn't good for her business. She used to tell me I should
never have happened. I was a mistake. That was in her better
moods. Otherwise, she shrieked at me and cursed the day I
was born. She said she couldn't count the number of times
she wished I'd die, but I was a tough kid. Too stubborn, I
guess." He stared into the fire. Abby wondered if he even

remembered they were in the same room. "I tried real hard to do what she wanted. Figured if I did then she'd be able to love me." He shook his head slowly. "Never could be good enough. I finally had to accept I never would."

He paused for a full minute and then continued, his voice so low Abby could barely make out his words.

"I always thought if she'd marry one of her boyfriends and settle down, we could have a real home. A home filled with. . ."

His voice trailed off, the sentence unfinished, but in her mind, Abby supplied the word, *Love,* and she recoiled as she felt the despair he acknowledged in admitting he felt himself unlovable.

It's not true.

She almost bolted from the chair, but caught herself just in time and forced herself to sit back and fold her hands in her lap. She felt Andrew's eyes upon her, but stared into the fire, afraid to look, knowing he would read what was in her heart. Her thoughts flared and a fire was kindled inside her.

For a brief moment, she'd seen him with his guard down. She wanted to tell him he wasn't unlovable. God loved him. God loved everyone. He needed to know that and believe it. It would surely chase away all the hurt his mother's words and actions had inflicted in his soul.

Andrew said, "God's love doesn't depend on how good we are. Or whether we deserve it. He gave us the ultimate gift of love—His own Son. It's up to us to choose what to do with it. We can't earn it. We simply have to believe it and accept it. Father taught us many verses like John 3:16, which says, 'For God so loved the world, that he gave his only begotten Son, that whosoever believeth in him should not perish, but have everlasting life.' And there's verses in Romans. 'For all have sinned, and come short of the glory of God,' and 'The wages of sin is death; but the gift of God is eternal life through Jesus Christ our Lord.' "

Andrew paused for a moment, watching Brewster's face, but his expression was unreadable.

Andrew continued, "There is nothing we can do to earn it. He gives it to us freely. We just have to accept it."

Abby saw hope flicker in Brewster's face, then wariness returned so quickly she wondered if what she saw was simply the reflection of the fire.

"It's easy to believe in love when that's all you've ever known." Brewster rose hastily to his feet and went to his bedroom, closing the door quietly behind him.

twelve

Abby pulled the covers over her ears in a vain attempt to block the sound of rain pummeling the roof, and the eaves weeping mournfully. Tonight the moon did not run silver fingers through her window and pull back the curtain of night. She wished for enough light to see the trees outside or to be able to stare at the Audubon prints on the wall. Even to see the shape of the logs so she could count how many were in each wall. Anything was preferable to the sounds inside her head—Lucy screaming her hatred to Brewster; venom-filled words ripping through her mind like gnarled fingers tearing at raw flesh. It was as if a huge canvas had been nailed to the wall next to her bed and Brewster's past slashed across it in blood and tears. The blood still dripped. The tears were still damp.

There had to be people who had known of Brewster's situation. Why had no one reached out a hand and helped?

Words raced through her mind. *Where was God?*

God is love. The words blasted through her mind.

She believed it with all her heart. Why then, didn't God do something? Why didn't He send someone?

He did. He sent you.

She sat bolt upright in bed and stared out the darkened window. Her! An instrument of God's love? Impossible. She couldn't do it. It was preposterous to think of loving Brewster. Wasn't it?

But was that what God was asking?

No, she decided. He was only asking her to show His love. To convince Brewster that love and healing were possible.

The argument continued unabated.

Did love stand a chance? Could she convince Brewster

135

there was love and healing for him? Did she really believe it was available for Brewster?

She lay back against her pillow and tugged the covers to her chin. Of course, she believed it. Without reservation.

But did she want to be the one responsible for carrying the message?

Again the sound of Lucy's words scraped through her mind. No child should ever hear that message; no person should believe those words.

God did love him. He forgave freely.

Could she show God's love without forgiving him?

She remembered a portion of Matthew's gospel and pulled her Bible toward her, grateful that Brewster had included it when he gathered up items back at the house for her and Andrew. Tipping it toward the light so she could read the words, she found what she was looking for in the sixth chapter, verses fourteen and fifteen, "For if ye forgive men their trespasses, your heavenly Father will also forgive you: But if ye forgive not men their trespasses, neither will your Father forgive your trespasses."

God had forgiven her. She had no choice but to forgive Brewster. She began to pray and as she did so, slowly her stubborn bitterness melted away.

A few minutes later, filled with a gentle peace, she opened her eyes. Now she could prove to Brewster that love existed. But she would need a plan.

The night deepened, the rain continued, and the rest of the house slept as Abby contrived her plan. Finally, she fell asleep, a smile on her lips.

She awoke still smiling and scurried from her bed, shivering in the early morning dampness. She paused to glance out the window and was relieved to see that, though the sky was still dark and lowering, it had stopped raining. The wet weather would give her a chance to implement her plan. She didn't want to waste any time.

She waited until Brewster was seated at the table before she poured his coffee. "I made it especially strong today," she announced, leaning over to fill his cup, balancing herself with one hand on his shoulder. "I noticed you like it that way." He twitched under her palm but she pretended not to notice. He'd soon get used to it. Since she had become aware of his nervousness at being touched, she had avoided it as much as possible. But not anymore. Touch was an important part of showing love.

Rather than set one place at each end of the table as had been her habit, this morning she set the two places so that she was on Brewster's right. He raised one eyebrow. Ignoring his look, she pulled out her chair and sat down.

"You know," she began, resting her hand lightly on his, "I really appreciate having flowers on the table every day. You must have to search to find so many of them."

He stared at her hand and when she didn't remove it, he flicked his arm away and picked up his spoon, becoming suddenly very busy stirring his porridge. "I'd have to be blind to miss them."

"Well, thank you anyway. They're especially cheery on a day like this."

He gulped his food and glanced out the window. "I think it's clearing. Sure hope so. There's a lot of work to be done." Dropping his spoon, he bolted for the door.

And you can't wait to escape, she thought, but she smiled sweetly and called, "Have a good morning," as he flung himself out the door.

She hummed as she worked, ignoring Andrew's slanted looks. It had been a good start to her plan, she decided.

When Brewster came in with a plump partridge, cleaned and ready for baking, she was ready. "I really appreciate this fresh meat all the time. You're a very good hunter."

"Comes with experience," he grunted and turned to leave.

"Wait," she called. "I just took these cookies from the oven. Help yourself." She extended a plate toward him.

He paused and studied her with eyes that burned, then he

nodded and took one.

All the things she found to say about him were true, but she had a feeling he had never heard them before. Or thought about them. He had never given himself credit for his abilities. And she intended he would never again be able to say he couldn't do anything that earned appreciation. Maybe Lucy had never seen and acknowledged his abilities, but Abby vowed she wouldn't be guilty of the same thing. And, as she looked for his abilities, she discovered there was much to appreciate.

He helped around the house, not only providing meat and flowers, but keeping the wood supply up and helping with Andrew's care. He was tidy. In fact, more tidy than either she or Andrew, and it made the housework easy.

That evening, she waited until he was preparing to read before she crossed the room to the bookshelves next to his chair.

"Which of these are your favorites?" she asked, running her fingers along the spines.

"They're all the same to me."

"You mean you enjoy this medical text?" she tipped the book, "as much as this collection of poems by Robert Browning?"

She held the leather-bound book, its cover soft with use, in the palm of her hand.

His eyes narrowed. "They serve entirely different roles. One is factual and informational. The other," he paused. "The other is like music. For the senses."

She handed him the book of poetry. "You must have a favorite."

Their eyes met—hers daring, his seemed to tell her she was playing with fire. *Fire doesn't have to be dangerous,* she thought. *It also warms and comforts.*

"Pass me that medical book." Andrew's voice snapped the spell. "Maybe it will tell me something about a broken leg. I can check up on Doc Baker. Make sure he knows what he's doing."

She pulled the book from the shelf and took it to him, then sat in the wine-colored armchair, turning her attention back to Brewster as he sat with his head bent over the pages, turning them slowly, pausing over the passages.

She stared at him until he looked up. "Do you have a favorite?"

He nodded.

"Would you read it aloud?" She held her breath as he continued to stare at her. She could feel him measuring her, wondering why she was doing this, wondering if she were mocking him or was genuinely interested. "I'd really enjoy it." She smiled, hoping he would see encouragement.

His eyes darkened until all she could see was the deep, bottomless void, and then he ducked his head. Softly at first, his voice growing stronger as he was caught up in the words, he read aloud.

His deep voice reverberated in her heart, and swept her away in a spell woven by the intertwining music of poetry and his deep tones. He finished with the words, " 'Ah, but a man's reach should exceed his grasp, or what's a heaven for?' "

Barely seeing him, her eyes focused on images floating like dreams. Finally he lifted his head and their eyes connected. A shock ran through her body, tingling her scalp. This was the first time he had allowed her a view of his soul and the vista before her was as wide and as vivid as the scene outside his door.

His heart flows with melody, she thought. *A man with such depth, such fineness, such capacity to love, and he refuses to believe in it.* Lucky would be the woman who was able to unlock that reservoir. She would be blessed with an endless bounty. Abby shivered, feeling empty and alone.

Why, she mused, should she feel alone? She would always have Andrew. She shifted her eyes. Her brother watched her with rapt attention, his book resting on his chest, his mouth agape. Andrew swallowed and blinked then flicked his gaze to Brewster.

Glad to be free of Andrew's stare, Abby picked up the book she had selected and opened its pages. She kept her eyes downward but the words floated before her eyes. She tingled with the power of the poetry. Absently, she turned a page, peeking out from under her eyelashes. Brewster too, had his head bent as if in deep concentration, but she guardedly watched him for several minutes and saw he did not turn a page. He looked up and caught her studying him. Their eyes locked. She searched for more of the depth she had caught a glimpse of, but found in its place only reluctance and misgiving. Whatever she had seen, or thought she'd seen, had vanished behind his perpetual shield, and as she tore her gaze away, a pang of disappointment made her sigh.

Andrew slammed his book shut and yawned loudly.

Abby felt a pang of guilt as she realized how long she had been lost in thought, completely unaware of how late it had grown. Perhaps Andrew would think it was because she had been caught up in her book. Maybe he failed to notice that she hadn't turned a page for a long time.

Brewster stretched and yawned. "I'm off to bed." He let his gaze slide over Abby, not quite meeting her eyes, before he strode purposefully to his room.

Before she went to bed, Abby penned a note to Sarah, hoping there would be a way of getting it delivered to Pine Creek. She told about Andrew's accident and needing to stay at Brewster's ranch, but skipped the part about the kidnapping. Later, she decided, when she could sit down with Sarah and explain it properly, she would tell the whole story. For now, she simply wanted to let Sarah know what was going on and ask for her prayers.

Brewster needs to know God's love, she wrote. *But his background doesn't make it easy for him to trust.*

She was sure Sarah would understand.

Later, in her bed, she lay staring up at the ceiling. She had counted the planks on the ceiling: thirty-five. She had studied the botanical prints, memorizing each detail until she could re-create them perfectly in her mind. She had measured the window and figured how many yards of fabric it would take to make three different styles of curtain. She tried to plan tomorrow's chores but couldn't get past breakfast. She counted slowly and lost track at twenty-five. She tried counting backwards and couldn't do it. She recited nursery rhymes, Bible verses, and hymns; but no matter what she did, her thoughts returned again and again to the same place. Brewster.

Brewster, her kidnapper. Her rescuer and protector.

Brewster, who brought flowers, filled his house with books and music, decorated his walls with fine artwork, and read poetry.

Brewster, neglected and probably mistreated by his mother, who vowed he did not believe in love.

How could he make this claim? She was sure he had a capacity to love as big as all outdoors.

She pursed her lips. It was up to her to make him see it.

&

The next morning, she determined again to implement her plan, but he shrugged out from under her hand as she poured his coffee, wolfed his breakfast before she could catch her breath, and bolted out the door.

There's more than one way to skin a cat, she mused, watching him stride across the grass.

She quickly completed her morning chores, then told Andrew that she needed some fresh air and headed outdoors, pausing as soon as both feet hit the ground. The rain had washed the colors so they sparkled like Monday's laundry. There were patches of scarlet, sunshine yellow, and freshwater blue of the wildflowers Brewster picked. The trees were variegated skeins of green. The damp earth breathed a warm, steamy breath. Abby lifted her face to the sky, filling her lungs until every pore was bathed in the clean pure air. Tipping her head, she listened, wondering where she would find Brewster.

She sauntered to the barn and stepped inside but found nothing but silent latticework shadows.

Turning to her right, she circled the corrals and almost missed him. The sound of chipping wood led her to the far end of the paddock, where Brewster squatted on his heels boring a hole in the bottom of a gatepost. A gate stood against the fence and she knew he was preparing to hang it.

He paused and glanced up as her shadow crossed. "You need something?" he asked, leaning his weight into the drill. Sawdust dribbled to his boots.

"No. Just enjoying the fresh air." Clasping her hands behind her, she watched him work.

He glanced at her out of the corner of his eye.

The silence stretching between them grew taut.

He pulled the bit out, shaking the shavings from it as he straightened. His gaze flashed over her face before he turned his attention to the next hole.

"I never have thanked you properly," she stammered, almost choking on the words as he turned to face her.

"For what?" His voice was deep and lazy.

"For finding Andrew and taking care of him. For letting us stay here while his leg mends."

He pushed himself upright from his knees and slowly turned the full force of his gaze upon her. He didn't speak. He simply looked at her with inscrutable sharpness.

It pressed her to fill the silence rather than meet his stare. "I mean I was really worried there for awhile when he was gone. I don't know what I would do if anything happened to him." She rushed on like a barrel rolling down the hill. "I remember a neighbor lady once telling me that if one twin dies, the other can't survive on its own. I guess it's the truth 'cause I know I couldn't survive without Andrew."

"Are you talking about death or just being apart?"

She couldn't look at him. She rubbed her thumb with her other hand and squeezed it until it turned white. "It feels the same either way."

"Seems to me there's a vast difference." He poised the bit against the post and began turning the handle.

"I didn't say there wasn't. I said it feels the same."

"You lost me."

"I don't expect you to understand. It's something special between twins." Her insides began to twist, and remembering how he had already questioned her relationship with Andrew, she wished she had kept her mouth shut. It seemed he was determined to see their twinness as a problem.

He stopped cranking the handle but stayed bent over his task, staring at the post. "Sounds to me like you're saying it would be impossible for you two to live apart. That you wouldn't be able to function. As I see it, things are bound to change."

"Why should they if we're both happy the way we are?"

"Does Andrew feel the same way? What happens if he wants to get married?"

"We'd work it out, I'm sure, but I don't see it's any concern of yours. I just wanted to thank you for your help."

"And so you did. It was nothing. I'd do it for anyone."

Clenching her hands at her sides, she glowered at him. Why must he be so difficult? She was simply trying to be friendly and polite and he had to treat her like a crackpot. Imagine treating her like she was the one who had a problem when it was he who couldn't trust people and didn't believe in love. The man had a real knack for drilling holes in offers of friendship, driving people away when they wanted to establish some sort of trust. Maybe she should just forget her plan. It would serve him right.

She stomped back to the house, pausing outside the door to collect her thoughts, knowing if she didn't smooth her face and calm her breathing Andrew would demand an explanation.

He's just jealous, she decided, because Andrew and she had always enjoyed the security of their love for each other. No doubt he would have liked to destroy it, and finding it wasn't possible, he was doing all he could to sully it.

Well, he could try as much as he liked. It would never work. She straightened her shoulders and lifted her chin. She would pay no attention to his remarks. She promised herself she would simply act like he hadn't said anything. Certainly she would never let him guess how much his words had stung.

It was easier than she thought to ignore Brewster when Dr. Baker called that afternoon.

"Well, well, well, and how is the patient today?" Dr. Baker bustled in and headed for Andrew with all the instincts of a homing pigeon. "I like the color of your leg. Very healthy looking." He widened his mouth into the shape of a smile, while nothing in his expression changed.

Abby had the feeling he was only pretending to smile to be polite but really found people quite challenging creatures. He seemed more comfortable dealing with a physical need, like Andrew's broken leg. She felt he would have been better pleased if he could have dealt with a leg without actually having to meet the whole person.

"I think it's time to see if this leg is going to do its stuff." He looked up as Brewster came in carrying a pair of crutches. "Good. Good. Here they are now. Let's get you up on these and see how you do."

Andrew swung his legs to the floor as Dr. Baker steadied him. Abby hurried to Andrew's side and she and the doctor helped him balance on his good leg.

"Aghh. My head feels like a top." Andrew grabbed her shoulder for support.

"Take it easy now. We won't rush things," Dr. Baker ordered.

In a few seconds, Andrew nodded that he was ready to continue.

"I don't want you putting any weight on this leg just yet. Got to give it a chance to heal. That was a nasty break you had. By the way, young man," he turned to Brewster. "Where'd you learn to set a bone like that?"

"Seen it done before," Brewster drawled, leaning against the door, watching the proceedings.

"These contraptions take a little getting used to. You put your weight here." The doctor showed Andrew how to use the crutches and helped him walk to the table and back.

"I'm shaking like a leaf," Andrew said and dropped to the sofa.

"Takes time. Takes time. No going out on the rough ground. Too dangerous. It's fine if you want to step outside, though. Just be careful. I think it's safe to take off this contraption." As he removed the splint, he talked, telling them news of the town. "I'll be back in a week. If things go well, we could think about you folks going home."

"Wait," Abby called as he headed for the door. "Could you give this to Sarah Fergusen for me?" She handed him the note she had written.

With a nod of his head the doctor agreed.

After he left, Abby stood looking down at Andrew. Home at last. It sounded so good. She wanted Andrew to share her joy, but she could see he was too tired. She lifted her head and caught Brewster staring at them. As soon as he saw her gaze, his expression hardened, but not before she caught a glimpse of something that made her wonder if he would miss them when they left.

thirteen

For three days after the doctor's visit, Andrew insisted on being outdoors every afternoon, promising he would not go further than the end of the path. Today he asked Abby to put a chair outside so he could sit and look at the sky and trees and mountains—things he had been missing more than he could stand. After she had him settled, Abby returned to the house where she prowled the rooms. Soon they would leave here and return to their own house—truly a simple cabin in comparison to this place. She had to admit she would miss many things about Brewster's house. The paintings, for sure. The garden scene had become her favorite, never failing to bring a rush of joy. The flowers on the table had come to mean so much to her that she had already decided to continue the habit once they were back home, though she didn't recall such a variety of flowers down the mountain.

Another thing she enjoyed was the variety of books. *I haven't even had time to examine all of them,* she thought with a pang as she ran her fingers along the shelves. As she surveyed the tidy shelf where her hand now rested, she noticed one book shoved in behind the others.

How strange. She had grown accustomed to the way Brewster kept his books in precise order.

She pushed aside the front books and pulled it out, turning it over in her hands. Across the spine was emblazoned *Holy Bible.* She stared at it in disbelief. *A Bible? Brewster has a Bible?* By the way he normally reacted when either she or Andrew mentioned God, she hadn't imagined he'd ever seen one, much less keep one in the house.

Opening the front cover, she saw an inscription penned in thick, black strokes:

To Brewster,
    We pray you will never forget we love you.
    Love never faileth.
    May the God of all peace be with you.

Mr. and Mrs. Rawson

She squeezed her eyes shut, then opened them to read the words again. There was no date but it was a plain, cloth-covered book much like the one she had received in Sunday school, and she thought he must have been a child when Mr. and Mrs. Rawson gave it to him.

Brewster said he didn't know anything about love, that he had never experienced it. Here was proof otherwise.

Dropping the Bible on the shelf, she raced out the front door.

"Where are you going?" Andrew called as she sped past him.

"For a walk."

"Looks more like a run. What's your hurry?"

"Nothing. I'll be back in a few minutes." She ran past the barn to the set of corrals that Brewster was building and skidded to a stop, breathing like a well-run horse.

Brewster faced her over the fence, his expression impassive.

"You said no one ever loved you. You said you didn't believe in love. What about the Rawsons?"

His eyebrows reached for his hair.

She rushed on. "I found a Bible in your bookcase and read the inscription. 'Never forget we love you.' The Rawsons must have loved you."

Brewster was busy weaving rails through parallel posts to make a section of fence and he bent to pick up another pole without answering.

"Well? What about the Rawsons?"

"They were just some people."

"What happened to them?"

"Nothing, as far as I know."

"You know what I mean."

He gave her an annoyed look. "We lost touch."

"You mean they moved?"

"No, we moved. We always moved."

"And they didn't write?"

"Nope."

"Why not?"

"Probably didn't know where to send a letter."

"Did you write them and let them know where you were?"

"Can't say as I did."

"You mean they're still waiting to hear from you?"

His dark look said it was none of her business, but she plowed on, determined to uncover this bit of mystery. "How long ago was that?"

"Years. Last saw them when I was ten or eleven."

"That's a long time for them to wait for a letter."

"I don't expect they are."

"So, who were they? How did you meet them? Tell me about them."

Clearly annoyed, he leaned the post against the existing fence and wiped his hands on his pants.

"They were just an old couple who lived across the back alley from the house where my mother worked."

"There has to be more to it than that." She crossed her arms to show that she wasn't leaving until he told her the whole story.

"They had this nice flower-filled yard. Behind us, like I said. It had a white picket fence around it. I used to sneak up to the fence and peak through the slats. I liked the flowers." He glared at her as if daring her to laugh.

She nodded. *You still like flowers,* she thought to herself.

"If I kept real quiet and hid behind the stalks, I could watch this white-haired old man weeding the garden. Sometimes an old lady helped him." His eyes looked past her, as green-shadowed as the shaded forest floor, full of history and memories normally hidden except when a flash of sunlight revealed their secrets. Abby knew he had forgotten she was standing there, but she didn't care. To see that ray of sunshine probe into the darkness of his memories and uncover something good was as sweet as finding a perfect orchid growing from the decay of long-dead leaves.

"I didn't think they knew I was there," he continued, his voice husky as distant, murmuring thunder. "But one day, the man was working in the corner and began talking to me.

" 'I see you're a fellow admirer of beauty. How many of these flowers can you name?'

"I didn't answer of course, but it didn't seem to matter. He just kept on talking.

"He went around the garden, naming all the flowers and telling me special things about each. 'These are called angel trumpets,' he said, pointing to some large white juglike flowers. 'Though Mother says they are more like death bells. They aren't her favorite flower, are they, Mother?'

"I hadn't seen the old lady come out of the house but there she was.

" 'Why, I see our young friend has come to visit and just in time for some iced tea. Come in and join us.' She pointed to the gate.

"I wasn't sure what to do. No one had ever invited me to anything before. But before I could find my voice, Mr. Rawson unlatched the gate and waved me in.

"After that I went over quite a lot. Mr. Rawson seemed anxious to teach me all about the garden and brought out books full of pictures and drawings."

Abby nodded again. Now she knew where his love for botany had been born. The prints in his bedroom convinced her that Mr. and Mrs. Rawson had not loved in vain. From them he had learned an appreciation for the beauties of nature that had nourished his deprived soul.

"When Mr. Rawson found out I couldn't read, he taught me. He was a preacher man so he used the Bible as my textbook." His expression hardened. Abby's breath stuck in her throat. She hated the way the sunshine faded from his eyes.

"One morning, Lucy said we were going and we did. That

was the end of that. I'd known all along it wouldn't last."

"Oh, no. That's where you're wrong." The kindness and love that these two old people had shown to a lost little boy touched her heartstrings. She wiped the corner of her eyes as she imagined how hurt they must have been by his disappearance. "You can't say their love didn't last when you never gave them a chance to tell you otherwise." How could he cast aside what they offered as easily as tossing out dishwater? "You never wrote them. You never let them know where you were. You just decided it was all a fake. You told yourself they never truly cared. Those poor old people. And you did the same with God. You decided you couldn't earn love and you wouldn't accept it as a gift. Even though the Rawsons proved otherwise, you act like everybody is like Lucy."

Her eyes ached with intensity, but when she saw the desperation in his eyes, she blinked aside her anger.

"Don't you think I wanted her to love me?" His voice rasped like a saw catching on a nail. "The only way I could survive was to tell myself I didn't care. And after awhile it was the truth."

The hollowness of his last words settled in her stomach like a lump of unbaked dough. Had he killed the part of him that was capable of giving and receiving love? She shook her head, unwilling to believe it. He still had a living, beating heart, flowing with the same needs and desires as everyone else. She was sure of it. There were so many things she saw as proof. Even her kidnapping had been a desperate means to fulfill those desires.

She knew he was equally, and stubbornly, convinced of the opposite. If only he could go back and repair some of the relationships from his past.

"Where's Lucy now?"

"I don't know and I don't care."

She glowered at him and he lowered his eyes.

"I heard she died," he mumbled.

"Where did you hear that?"

"From some saddle tramp. Probably one of her customers."

If it were true, then all hope of mending that relationship was gone.

"Where do you suppose the Rawsons are now?"

" 'Spect they're still in the same place. Richmore."

"Why don't you write them?"

"Now?" His eyes widened momentarily before he narrowed them to a slit.

She nodded. "I bet they're still praying for you and hoping someday you'll write."

"Yeah, sure. I can see them going to the post office every day checking for a letter from some little kid they knew pretty near twenty years ago."

"Don't be flippant. You know what I mean."

He bent to pick up the maul. "It would be a waste of time." He swung the hammer over his head and brought it down on the top of the post, shutting the door to any further questions.

Abby watched him pound the post into place. *How many minutes does it take to write a letter?* She wanted to knock the heavy hammer from his hand and shout the question in his face. So what if he had to take a risk? He had to take a chance once in awhile in order to gain what he really wanted and she was sure she knew what he wanted. To be loved—completely, unconditionally, unquestioningly, through good and bad, day in and day out.

She could love him like that. She gasped and grabbed the gate for support. She loved him exactly like that. She wanted to grab him by the neck and pull his face down to hers and say the words so plain and simple he couldn't misunderstand.

I love you, Brewster Johnson.

She turned and stumbled away, lest he see the blaze in her face. It was useless, she told herself. Even if she could bring herself to say the words, he would never allow them to reach his brain, let alone his heart. Blindly, she followed the trail past the barn.

When had she fallen in love with him? So many scenes

filled her mind: The beauty of his house and the certainty that it was an expression of the real Brewster. Brewster setting Andrew's leg. The jar full of flowers on the table every day. His dark head bent over a book of poetry. His fury exploding into action as he rescued her from Petey and Sam.

Yes, she admitted, she had felt something for him even then. When he risked his life for her she knew he was a man who would be prepared to die for her. That's when she had first realized he was a man who was worth loving.

Why then had it taken so long for her to realize the truth?

She supposed it was partly because he made it so plain he didn't want love. He tried so desperately to convince everyone. She wondered if he had succeeded in convincing himself.

She skidded to a stop under the pine trees and turned to watch him as he worked. He paused to wipe his brow, then gathered himself and lifted the maul again.

She stood for a long time under the trees. The scent of pine needles mingled with memories of her past ordeal—once so terrifying, but now almost precious when viewed from the vantage point of love. If only she could make him believe in love.

She hugged her arms around her. How would it feel to be loved by this man? To share a faith in Jesus Christ. To fight the elements side by side and carve out a place in this beautiful land. To have someone she could truly give her heart to. She had no doubt that once Brewster gave his heart it would be well and truly given. She allowed her imagination to soar until she could see his house filled with love, a baby in her arms, another at her feet. Her legs grew rubbery, and she sighed.

Until he allowed God's love into his heart she knew he would not be ready for the kind of relationship she ached for. Without a shared faith, all her hopes and dreams were useless.

Please, God, work in his life. Help him to accept Your love.

Even if Brewster never loved her, she knew he needed the healing power of God's love.

She started back toward the house.

If only he would believe in love.

fourteen

"You're fit as a fiddle," the doctor said, slamming his bag shut. "Go on home and behave yourself. You're one lucky lad, you know. Most legs broken as bad as that one was would never be good as new again."

"You mean I'm all mended?" Andrew asked, his voice revealing his surprise.

"Throw away the crutches, boy. You might find your leg a little sore at first, but take it easy and you'll be fine."

Andrew stared at him a moment longer, then tossed the crutches at his feet and whooped. "We're going home, Abby." He limped to her side and grabbed her hands. "I can get our place ready for winter and begin breaking the horses I bought. About time, too."

Dr. Baker shook his head and smiled his paper-thin smile. "Take it easy, son."

Andrew nodded, but his grin threatened to split his face in two.

Abby managed a wan smile, but she knew her effort was wobbly. She was overjoyed that Andrew was better and she was ready to be in her own home again, but her pleasure was marred by Brewster's stubborn indifference. Avoidance was more like it. She hadn't been able to break through his tough veneer and convince him to believe in love. More than once she had almost blurted out the words, *I love you,* but no good opportunity had arisen, and something told her that he wouldn't believe her anyway. And now, if they left, when would she have another chance?

It wasn't that she hadn't tried. The evenings had been long and warm, and they had spent many hours reading and discussing things. Having discovered that both Andrew and

153

Abby enjoyed it, Brewster often read bits of poetry aloud. Andrew, especially, had taken every opportunity to tell Brewster about God's unconditional love, and Abby had added her agreement, but Brewster remained adamant. He'd survived so far, he insisted, and he wasn't about to change.

"It's too hot in here. I'm going for a walk," Abby announced, her fingers clutching the letter Dr. Baker had brought from Sarah. As she strode down the path, she was aware that Andrew was watching her intently. She'd caught him studying her often in the past few days and she knew he was attuned to her inner turmoil. Unfortunately, he was as powerless as she to do anything. Thank goodness he didn't feel it necessary to say something. Knowing that he knew and understood comforted Abby. She knew he wanted only to see her happy because that was what she wanted for him. She had tried to explain that to Brewster but his doubts about their dependency on each other never faltered.

It's simply another way of shutting himself away, she thought with startling clarity. In the face of Abby and Andrew's love for each other, Brewster determined it excluded others. She wondered if he really did have feelings for her and was using this argument as protection.

A spark of hope stirred inside her and she hurried down the path in search of him, determined to convince him that love was available for him.

As she followed the narrow ribbon of the wagon trail, Abby thought about a future without Brewster and saw it as gloomy as the dust-mottled leaves of the trees.

But even worse than her own sense of loss was the sorrow of Brewster's self-enforced loneliness in refusing to accept love. Not only her love for him, but more importantly, God's love for him. She wanted to wrap her understanding of God's full and free love in a gift box and hand it to Brewster. *If he would only open the box, God's love would flood his soul and melt his heart.*

Sighing, she wiped the beads of sweat from her forehead

and admitted her powerlessness to change his hardened heart. She had hoped that forcing Brewster to acknowledge a love for her would erase his pain and enable him to accept God's gift of love.

Only God could do that!

Hope blossomed anew. Nothing was too hard for God and she closed her eyes and prayed for Him to break through Brewster's strong defenses.

"That he might know the strength of Your love," she whispered.

As she hurried on, the heat of the day was a heavy blanket on her shoulders. *If only there was a cool breeze.* She lifted her hair off her neck and poked it back into a bun, securing it with the few hairpins she hadn't lost. Heat waves shimmered across the face of the mountains. Underfoot, the grass crackled. A thudding sound in the distance made her back teeth tighten.

A trail parted the trees and she turned under the shade, but even there the heat clung to her. A few feet more and she came to an open field. Across the clearing she saw Brewster, his back to her, his shirt off as he set posts for a fence. His stance wide, he braced himself and dug a hole with an auger, his back muscles rippling and his biceps bulging with the effort. Sweat rolled down his bronzed back. Dropping the auger, he reached out a gloved hand, snagged a post, and dropped it into the hole. Widening his stance again, he grasped the handle of the heavy maul with both hands. The muscles in his arms bulged and his back muscles swelled and corded into a deep vee. Abby marveled at the crescendo of power as he swung the hammer over his head and slammed the top of post. She saw the hammer bounce before she heard the thud. Her legs quivered.

He dropped the maul to the ground and as he turned to grab the next post he saw her. He leaned forward, catching his breath, his hands resting on the handle. He didn't say anything. She knew he couldn't, or wouldn't. He had to maintain his posture of indifference. But she was convinced that his facade hid a dawning knowledge of her love for him, and she was equally certain that the feelings were mutual. She knew that it scared him to death, because it would make him vulnerable. She had to convince him that love was worth breaking down his brick wall. Without love, his heart would remain forever an empty void.

Her legs unsteady, she walked toward him.

Every detail of his features seemed magnified as she drew closer—the dark shadow that his whiskers drew along his chin, the way his hair clung in damp tendrils to his neck, the trail of sweat trickling down his chest over sun-kissed skin. She stopped her eyes from trailing further down his chest and felt her cheeks turn to fire.

He pulled a rag from his back pocket and wiped his face.

"Pretty hot, isn't it?" she murmured, her tongue thick.

"A mite."

"Hard work for a day like this."

"One day's the same as the next."

Something inside her exploded. "Why do you do that?"

He raised his eyebrows. "Didn't notice I was doing anything."

"You always act like you've got no feelings. You don't feel heat. Or cold. Or pain. Or love." The words dropped into the heat like hailstones.

His jaw tightened. "I just tell the truth." He lifted a canteen from the ground and took a deep drink.

A drop of water trickled down his chin onto his chest. The words that had been forming in her mind disappeared in a flush of longing. If only he would admit that he loved her and take her into his arms. She understood that somehow accepting her love and believing in God's love were intertwined. She knew she could never give herself fully to this man until he had found his way to God, yet she longed for things that could not be. Blinking, she forced her thoughts back to what she wanted to say.

"You don't know the truth." Would he hear it if she told him? She rushed on before he could answer. "I don't know about Lucy. Maybe she loved you. Maybe she didn't. I do know that if a mother doesn't love her child, it is the mother who is sick. Not the child." She held up her hand to stop him from interrupting. "And I do know the Rawsons loved you. And I know God loves you." She took a deep breath and faced him squarely, her eyes refusing to let him look away. "And I love you." Her firm, solid words rang across the pasture and disappeared into the trees. He stared at her, the expression in his eyes never changing even though a muscle along his cheek twitched. With a dismissive wave, he turned to pick up an iron bar and began tamping the dirt around the post.

She stared at his bent head, anger and embarrassment raging a war. "Brewster." She touched his arm and heat raced up her fingers.

"I don't want to hear it," he growled.

"Hear what? That somebody loves you? Does that shoot holes in your self-protective beliefs? How are you going to insist you don't believe in love when the evidence is standing right in front of you?" She placed herself squarely between Brewster and the post, her arms jammed on her hips.

He straightened his back and met her eyes. His eyes were as cold as stone. "I guess we all have our hangups, don't we?" His voice was like tumbling gravel.

"I don't." Bright lights flashed through her brain.

"Yep. You do." His voice slow and lazy. "You talk about God and how much he loves you. But it ain't God you depend on. It's Andrew. If something happened to Andrew, I wonder. Would you still believe in love?"

Her jaw dropped and she stared at him. How could he possibly have misunderstood? Yes, she'd said she couldn't imagine life without Andrew, but she hadn't meant it would make her doubt God's love. She knew God loved her. Why was Brewster always harping back to the subject of Andrew and

Abby? It was like he couldn't believe they truly cared about each other.

Suspicion germinated in her mind. Was he jealous? Did he think love for one person excluded love for a second? Did he think Abby's love for him would play second fiddle to her love for Andrew?

She grabbed his shoulder and forced him to look at her again. "You don't understand," she whispered. "Love doesn't divide when you love another; it multiplies. Don't you see?"

Something flashed behind his eyes and she held her breath, waiting for him to soften, but the hardness descended and he shook his head.

"There's nothing to see. Love doesn't last. It's not real."

"Brewster, that's just not true. You've told yourself lies and believed them for so long, you're convinced they're true. But believing a lie doesn't make it true."

He picked up the auger and bar in one hand, and with the other grasped the handle of the maul, and walked toward the next fence post a few feet away.

Abby watched him until he set the auger in the ground and began turning it. He never looked back. The rigid set of his shoulders told her he wouldn't.

A lump the size of a large rock settled in the pit of her stomach and Abby turned and retraced her steps to the house, admitting defeat. She had tried to prove to him that love was worth believing in and she had failed. There was nothing left but to pack her few things and return home to pick up the threads of the joy and peace she had known before she met Brewster.

She was almost back to the cabin when she remembered Sarah's letter and pulled it out of her pocket.

Dear Abby,
   I was shocked to hear all that's happened to you.
Not a very warm welcome to your new home, I fear.
I know little about Mr. Johnson. I did not even

know his given name until you told me in your letter.
He sounds a very lonely man. I know he appears
rather unsociable when he comes to town but I'm
sure he has his reasons.

I'm continuing to pray for you and for healing for
Andrew's leg. May God give you strength and wisdom
and do His work in Brewster Johnson's life.

Abby folded the page and dropped it back in her pocket. They were the words of encouragement and direction she needed. She would trust God to do the work needed. Humming, she returned to the house.

≈

Abby leaned against the window, staring at the mountains. Somewhere high in their invincible heights was Brewster's house. She knew it lay south of the saw-toothed peak but she couldn't pinpoint the exact location.

She let her eyes drift down the deep green of the pine forest to the aspen woods closer to the cabin she and Andrew shared. It still surprised her to see the leaves dancing in their flashy golden gowns. A blue jay parted the leaves and disappeared.

"Abby?" Andrew's voice broke into her thoughts. "Are you all right?"

She wondered if he had spoken before and she hadn't heard. Without turning, she nodded. "It's just the season. Fall is so melancholic."

"You're really missing him, aren't you?"

She turned, letting her back rest against the wall. Brown eyes met brown eyes. "Yes, I suppose I am." They had never spoken directly about it. Hadn't needed to. Andrew had seen for himself the way Brewster stood stiff and cold in the open door of his house when they had said good-bye and thanked him for his help. Andrew, feeling Abby's misery, had taken her hand and helped her onto the horse.

"Maybe he'll change his mind," he said now.

"I don't think so." Brewster had what he wanted—a place in the mountains where no one would ever invade his privacy. And a barred heart that allowed no one to share his emotions. He'd had a chance to choose otherwise and had chosen not to. Abby had to live with the reality that Brewster could not—or would not—allow love to enter his life.

"You never know." Andrew rose from the table. "In the meantime I've got work to do." He paused at the door until she nodded.

Long after he was gone, she sat staring at the dirty dishes. Even after all she had eaten, Abby still felt as hollow and empty as a rain barrel during a drought. She knew the hungry emptiness could not be filled with food. It was Brewster-shaped. And she knew it would never be filled. How then was she to deal with the stirring inside that leaped at the sound of a horse riding into the yard, or the outer door opening, yet curled into a knot when it was only Andrew? How was she to stop her heart from fluttering at the scent of pine needles? Or when she caught the brightness of a patch of wildflowers? How was she to silence the unending wail of pain burrowing into her soul?

Shaking her head to clear her thoughts, she slowly gathered up the dishes and lowered them into the hot, soapy water. When she had finished, she went to her room.

Brewster had been right about one thing. She had never before separated God's love and Andrew's love in her mind—until recently, when she found Andrew's love was not enough to ease her pain. She opened her Bible and began reading where she had left off yesterday. The only thing that helped ease her pain was casting herself on God's love. Reading her Bible had become a balm to her bleeding heart.

She finished the portion she had chosen and bent her head in prayer, asking God to heal her wounds.

As peace stole into her heart, she set aside the Bible and knelt in front of the trunk where she had left her winter things. Cold weather would soon be upon them and she needed to be prepared. She removed a gray wool dress that had been her favorite last year. The color made her feel warm and alive and she admitted it was because the soft gray made her hair glow with rich highlights. Beneath it lay a black skirt and two flannel nighties. She shook them out and laid them on the bed. Returning to the trunk, her fingers touched something hard and cold. She pulled out a framed picture of Father in front of their house in England. She had forgotten it in her excitement of unpacking and settling into her new home in a new country. She pressed her finger to his likeness. The old country seemed so far away, another lifetime. She was glad Father wrote regularly to assure them he was well and happy.

Smiling, she withdrew a bundle of material from the trunk. She'd been saving these pieces for a quilt—an English Wedding Ring quilt like one her mother had owned. She loved the colors and textures of cloth and was suddenly glad to have this project to help pass the long winter days ahead.

Unfolding the material, she caressed the soft, brown flannel from which she had made shirts for Father and Andrew two winters ago. There were pieces from her gray dress and her pink print nighties. She rubbed a bit of heavy, green brocade between her fingers. Mrs. Olsen had given her that. She folded back some more pieces and gasped, falling back on her heels.

She'd completely forgotten the scrap she had tucked into this bundle so it wouldn't be damaged or lost. Slowly, almost not breathing, she withdrew it as her thoughts fled back to the day she had discovered it.

She could no longer remember why she had gone to the attic. Nor what she was looking for. Or why she had chosen that particular trunk to look through. What she did remember as clearly as if it happened this morning was discovering the square of blue cloth. It was the color of deep, calm water, rich and smooth, the finest quality wool Abby had ever seen. It felt like velvet between her fingers, soft as a cat's fur, and she caressed it hungrily. But her mind hadn't been on the bit of cloth. Rather it had flooded with memories. She had been crying about some small injury. Seems like it was a bump on the head. Gentle arms had pulled her to a comforting lap and pressed her head to a warm breast. She could feel a lullaby beneath her ear and smell roses. And she had pressed her face into warm, soft, blue material. Exactly like the scrap she had found.

It was the only real memory she had of her mother and she had taken the square of blue and hidden it under her pillow, clutching it in her fingers before she fell asleep. As she grew older, she had tucked it safely in the top drawer of her bureau right next to the small photo of her mother. Only on really bad days did she pull it out and bury her face in its softness as she did now. She breathed its soothing familiarity as tears flowed unchecked, soaking the cloth while the smell of wet wool wrapped about her.

She cried for a mother she could barely remember and who could not comfort her now, when she needed it most. And she cried for a love that would never be because another mother, whose arms had never comforted, had left behind a legacy of fear and mistrust rather than the gentle, warm memory she had.

fifteen

Abby stood at the clothesline, the wind tearing at her skirt, biting her skin. She glanced at the sky, half expecting to see snow, then turned her attention back to getting the clothes off the line before her fingers froze. It was only October. *Surely,* she thought as she struggled with the wind-whipped articles, it won't snow this early. But Andrew had warned her that winter came early in the foothills.

"I'm told that it often snows much sooner than this." He'd shaken his head, but when she asked if he was sorry they'd chosen this particular place, he had brightened. "Nope," he said. "Still the prettiest bit of land I ever saw."

She had nodded and agreed.

Yet there were times she wished they'd chosen a spot to the south, or perhaps to the north. Anyplace where Brewster's path wouldn't have crossed hers. Over and over she reminded herself she would never see him again, but she hadn't been able to silence the longing in her heart.

She continued to pray for God to send healing into his heart and consoled herself that whether she ever saw him again or not, God would work in his life.

Dropping the sheets in the basket, she picked it up and turned toward the house. Her hair, tugged loose by the teasing wind, blew across her face and obstructed her view. Balancing the load on her hip, she scooped her hair back and almost dropped her basket. The wind sucked away her startled scream.

Not fifteen feet away stood Brewster, twisting his hat in his hands, the wind sifting through his hair.

She couldn't speak. She couldn't breathe. The basket creaked as she clutched it in her arms. She blinked, expecting him to disappear, but he was still there, his feet planted firmly on the ground. She let her glance skim over his face then ducked her head, hoping against hope he was real, yet afraid it was only her imagination running wild. How often in her thoughts had she heard his voice across the yard? Or looked up, thinking it was his footsteps. Slowly, her heart pounding in her ears, she raised her head and looked deep into his uncertain eyes.

"Have you come to kidnap me again?"

"No." A spear of darkness flashed through his eyes. "I have something to show you," he growled.

Nodding, she moved toward him. "Come to the house. It's too cold out here." He took the basket from her as he turned. Together they crossed the yard. Neither spoke until the door closed behind them.

"I'll take that." She set the basket by the stove before she faced him. Now that the initial shock of seeing him had passed, she studied him, drinking in every detail. His hair was a little longer, strands of it blown across his cheek. Her fingers twitched, longing to catch them and tuck them into place. His face seemed leaner, but it was more than a little thinness that made him seem different and she strained to grasp the difference. It was something in his expression, she decided. Something hovering just beyond her grasp. His eyes, too, were different. *Almost inviting,* she thought, and knew it was only her own desperate longings making her see something that wasn't there.

He cleared his throat, the sound snapping her out of her preoccupation.

"Have a seat while I make coffee." She nodded toward the table.

"Thanks." He sat on the edge of the wooden chair, twisting his hat between his fingers.

"It's a cold day for a ride," she said, trying to fill the silence.

"It'll get colder." He glanced around the room. "Where's Andrew?"

"Gone to bring the horses closer to home. He's worried it will snow."

"Feels like it could." He set his hat on the table and then seemed to think better of it and picked it up again.

She filled two cups and placed them on the table, and sat on the chair across from him. She couldn't quit looking at him, filling her mind with the shape of his brow, the slash across his cheek, the jut of his jaw. She wanted to gather enough looks to last the long winter.

"I did what you said."

She started in her chair, surprised by his voice. She'd been so busy stocking her larder of memories that she'd forgotten his reason for being here. Not that it mattered. It was enough that he was there, if only for a few minutes to conduct an errand. But she couldn't remember saying he should do something. "What did I say?" Only part of her mind was on the question.

"About writing the Rawsons."

"Oh, yes." Guess she had said something of the sort, but all she could think right now was how soft his eyes were, how dark the fringe of eyelashes.

"They were still in the same place. They wrote me a reply." He waited, but when she didn't answer, he continued. "You want to read the letter?" Pulling an envelope from his breast pocket, he offered it to her.

The sound of paper rattling forced her back to reality. She let her gaze linger on his strong mouth a heartbeat longer, then blinked away her dreams. "Thank you." She pulled out three sheets of well-thumbed pages and read the words slowly. It was as she guessed. The Rawsons wrote they had never stopped praying for him. Their greatest desire was that he would remember what they had told him about God and His love and not forget their love. She flipped a page and continued to read the bits of news. Mr. Rawson had recently celebrated his seventieth birthday and could no longer look after the flowers as well as he wanted. Somehow she had assumed that the Rawsons had been in their seventies at the time

Brewster knew them, but then she realized that to a youngster anyone past the age of sixteen was old.

Abby gasped as she read the next line. Lucy had come back in the hope that the Rawsons would know where to locate Brewster. Lucy had tried to find Brewster before she died.

By the time Abby reached the end of the letter, her vision was so blurred she could barely make out the words.

"Oh, Brewster. What a lovely letter."

"You were right. They prayed for me all those years." His face grew serious. "Lucy knew it was the only place I would ever return to. That's why she went back when she knew she was dying. I can't believe she tried to get a message to me."

"She did get a message to you." She blinked back the tears and read from the last page.

" 'Your mother made us promise we would give you this message if we ever got a chance. She even asked us to write it down so we would get it right, so these are her exact words. She said, 'Tell Brewster I know I wasn't much of a mother. He was a good kid. He deserved better.' ' "

Abby's voice shook so much, she had to stop. "I'm so glad for you," she whispered when she could speak again.

He nodded. "When I got this letter, it set me to thinking about some of the things you said."

She had said a lot of things and thought even more. Things such as how compelling his eyes were when they flashed shards of green like they were now; how she longed to feel his hair, knowing it was silky and smooth; how warm his skin looked, like it carried the touch of summer sun. But she had never said those words aloud and she couldn't think what things he was referring to.

"You kept hounding me that I had to be willing to give love a chance."

She wouldn't have called it hounding, but yes, she had challenged him not to throw love away.

"You said love was worth a few risks."

I would gamble my life for a chance to share your love, she thought, her eyes lingering on his lips, fascinated with the way they formed each syllable.

"I thought about that lots," he continued. "That's why I wrote that letter in the first place." He arched back in his chair and lurched to his feet to pace the floor. "I'd shut myself up. I figured if I didn't believe in love, I'd never be hurt or disappointed that no one loved me."

Turning, he strode back to the table and stared down at her. "Then you said what you did."

"What did I say?"

"You know." His gaze settled on something above her head. "What you said about loving me." His voice dropped to deep within his chest and she strained to catch the words.

He stood so close she could smell sawdust and pine needles. Her throat constricted so her words were a mere whisper. "What I said was, I love you."

"Yeah. And I didn't know what to say or do. I didn't know how to feel." He was pacing again, crossing the room in long strides and spinning on his heel to return.

It wasn't hard to know what to do, or say, she wanted to scream at him. *All you had to do was pull me into your arms and promise me you'd love me until forever.* She couldn't sit any longer. His pacing made her feel like exploding. She hurried to the fireplace, pressing her back to the cold rocks and turned to watch him.

He rubbed his jaw. "After you and Andrew left, I was so alone. I kept telling myself I'd get used to being alone again. But I didn't. I even thought of riding over."

"Why didn't you? You knew you'd be welcome." A hollow ache echoed in her chest. So many times she had stood at the window wishing he'd come. She wanted to tell him, to repeat her vow of love. But she couldn't. She still didn't know why he had come, or what he wanted. It seemed there was more on his mind, yet he seemed unable to say what it was.

"I knew you'd be hospitable but I was too confused. I had to sort out all that stuff twisted up inside me."

"Such as?" Narrowing her eyes, she wondered what he meant.

"Why wasn't I loved by my mother?"

"It wasn't your fault."

"It's easy to say that. I told myself the same thing all the time. But it didn't help." He ceased his pacing and stood directly in front of her, his eyes boring into hers.

There was an expression in his eyes she couldn't fathom and she tore her gaze away, uncertain where to look. Finally she settled for looking at the letter where it lay on the table.

"The letter helped, didn't it?" she asked, understanding suddenly that the words contained in it had helped him sort out some of his confusion.

Something warm and eager flashed across his face. "Yes. It was like a door had been stuck for years and finally swung open. When I read her message, all of a sudden I remembered all sorts of little things. Like wherever we went there was someone who watched over me—usually the barkeep. And I can see now that Lucy sent me to that person." His voice rang with freedom. "I think it was her way of seeing I was kindly treated. It was the only way she knew of taking care of me."

He paused. "I know now she did the best she could for me. I never saw it that way before."

Abby could see he was bursting.

"It's like my whole life has been filled with closed doors that suddenly opened wide. I saw all the good times I'd had at the Rawsons. I remembered how special I felt. How good it had been when they told me God loved me." His eyes shone like the sun was trapped behind them. "I began reading the Bible. I found so many answers there." He straightened and shook his head as if to clear his thoughts. "I can't tell you how much my heart has changed." His expression hardened ever so slightly. "Sometimes I'm afraid it's too good to be true and I don't deserve it." He strode away and stood with his back to her.

She half stepped toward him, then stopped. Clasping her

hands in front of her, she spoke softly to his back, "How many of us deserve the love we're given? Sometimes we accept it. Sometimes we don't." She still didn't know how far he'd come in accepting it himself. Had he healed enough to believe in her love?

"I still have so much to sort out." Slowly, he turned toward her. "Remember what you said to me?" He took a step toward her.

She shook her head. How could she know what he meant?

A waiting, longing expression filled his eyes and then she knew. A tiny bubble of joy began to swell upward from the pit of her stomach. "Brewster Johnson, I love you yesterday, now, and forever." Her smile reached for her ears.

His eyes filled with flashes of happiness. He took another step toward her until they could have touched each other, but neither did. Brewster's mouth opened and closed and then he said, "I have something I want to say to you." His voice was so deep it plucked chords of pleasure in her chest. His Adam's apple plunged up and down as he struggled for the words he wanted. "Abigail Landor," he began, "I love you." The tension drained from his face.

Knowing how difficult it was for him to say these words aloud, Abby found them extra sweet. Her bubble of joy exploded in a shout of laughter and she flung herself at him. He caught her in his arms and crushed her to his chest where she heard a rumble of laughter. She couldn't remember hearing him laugh before and she tipped her head back to watch as his face creased in a smile that transformed his whole countenance. She was reminded of the way the early sunshine flashed off the mountains, filling them with diamond-sharp brightness.

He looked deeply into her eyes, searching them in a way he had never done before. "There's still a lot I have to work out," he warned.

"I know." And she did something she'd wanted to do for such a long time. She lifted a finger and trailed it along his jawline, thrilling at the roughness of his whiskers.

He caught her hand and pressed her palm to his lips, his eyes never leaving her face.

"I'm not very good at this loving business. I don't know how to go about it."

Her other hand sought the back of his neck where she could tangle her fingers in his silky locks. "I'll help you all I can." She lifted her face toward him.

He gave a sound halfway between a gasp and a sigh before he lowered his head, catching her lips with his. He held her so tight she could barely breathe, but she didn't mind. She wrapped her arms around his shoulders and allowed the kiss to start fires inside her. Her toes were tingling and her knees were shaking when he lifted his head.

He had a smile that would melt snow, she decided.

Suddenly his eyes clouded and he softened his grasp on her. "What about my scar?"

"What about it?" She trailed a finger from where it began at his bottom eyelid to where it puckered to an end just above his lower jaw.

"You don't find it repulsive?"

Her fingers stopped moving and she stepped back, forcing him to drop his arms to his side. "Brewster Johnson. How dare you ask me that!"

He looked sheepish but his eyes remained insistent.

She grasped his face between her hands and met his eyes boldly. "I think this scar has become a symbol for you. A physical reminder not to trust love." She pulled his face closer. "From now on." She began to trail kisses along his cheek. "I want you to see it as a reminder of how much I love you." She continued to kiss his scar line. "Consider it a flag of love."

A deep rumble filled his chest as he swept her into his arms and covered her face with kisses.

"I have so much to learn," he murmured against her mouth.

She enjoyed the touch of his lips a moment longer, then broke away long enough to whisper, "But what fun to learn together."

A Letter To Our Readers

Dear Reader:

In order that we might better contribute to your reading enjoyment, we would appreciate your taking a few minutes to respond to the following questions. When completed, please return to the following:

Rebecca Germany, Managing Editor
Heartsong Presents
PO Box 719
Uhrichsville, Ohio 44683

1. Did you enjoy reading *Unchained Hearts?*
   ❑ Very much. I would like to see more books
      by this author!
   ❑ Moderately
      I would have enjoyed it more if _____

   _____

2. Are you a member of **Heartsong Presents**? ❑ Yes ❑ No
   If no, where did you purchase this book? _____

   _____

3. What influenced your decision to purchase this
   book? (Check those that apply.)

   ❑ Cover   ❑ Back cover copy

   ❑ Title   ❑ Friends

   ❑ Publicity   ❑ Other _____

4. How would you rate, on a scale from 1 (poor) to 5
   (superior), the cover design? _____

5. On a scale from 1 (poor) to 10 (superior), please rate the following elements.

   ___Heroine   ___Plot

   ___Hero   ___Inspirational theme

   ___Setting   ___Secondary characters

6. What settings would you like to see covered in **Heartsong Presents** books?_____

   _____

   _____

7. What are some inspirational themes you would like to see treated in future books?_____

   _____

   _____

8. Would you be interested in reading other **Heartsong Presents** titles?   ❑ Yes   ❑ No

9. Please check your age range:
   ❑ Under 18   ❑ 18-24   ❑ 25-34
   ❑ 35-45   ❑ 46-55   ❑ Over 55

10. How many hours per week do you read? _____

Name _____

Occupation_____

Address_____

City_____ State_____ Zip_____

·····Hearts♥ng·····

Any 12 *Heartsong Presents* titles for only $26.95 *

*plus $1.00 shipping and handling per order and sales tax where applicable.

HISTORICAL ROMANCE IS CHEAPER BY THE DOZEN!

Buy any assortment of twelve *Heartsong Presents* titles and save 25% off of the already discounted price of $2.95 each!

HEARTSONG PRESENTS TITLES AVAILABLE NOW:

·········· Presents ········

__HP216 BLACK HAWK'S FEATHER,
          Carolyn R. Scheidies
__HP219 A HEART FOR HOME, *Norene*
          Morris
__HP220 SONG OF THE DOVE, *Peggy Darty*
__HP223 THREADS OF LOVE, *Judith*
          McCoy Miller
__HP224 EDGE OF DESTINY, *Darlene*
          Mindrup
__HP227 BRIDGET'S BARGAIN, *Loree Lough*
__HP228 FALLING WATER VALLEY, *Mary*
          Louise Colln
__HP235 THE LADY ROSE, *Joyce Williams*
__HP236 VALIANT HEART, *Sally Laity*
__HP239 LOGAN'S LADY, *Tracie J. Peterson*
__HP240 THE SUN STILL SHINES, *Linda*
          Ford
__HP243 THE RISING SUN, *Darlene Mindrup*
__HP244 WOVEN THREADS, *Judith McCoy*
          Miller

__HP247 STRONG AS THE REDWOOD,
          Kristin Billerbeck
__HP248 RETURN TO TULSA, *Norma Jean*
          Lutz
__HP251 ESCAPE ON THE WIND, *Jane*
          LaMunyon
__HP252 ANNA'S HOPE, *Birdie L. Etchison*
__HP255 KATE TIES THE KNOT, *Loree Lough*
__HP256 THE PROMISE OF RAIN, *Sally*
          Krueger
__HP259 FIVE GEESE FLYING, *Tracie*
          Peterson
__HP260 THE WILL AND THE WAY,
          DeWanna Pace
__HP263 THE STARFIRE QUILT, *Alice Allen*
__HP264 JOURNEY TOWARD HOME,
          Carol Cox
__HP267 FOR A SONG, *Kathleen Scarth*
__HP268 UNCHAINED HEARTS, *Linda Ford*

Great Inspirational Romance at a Great Price!

Heartsong Presents books are inspirational romances in contemporary and historical settings, designed to give you an enjoyable, spirit-lifting reading experience. You can choose wonderfully written titles from some of today's best authors like Peggy Darty, Sally Laity, Tracie Peterson, Colleen L. Reece, Lauraine Snelling, and many others.

When ordering quantities less than twelve, above titles are $2.95 each.
Not all titles may be available at time of order.

SEND TO: Heartsong Presents Reader's Service
         P.O. Box 719, Uhrichsville, Ohio 44683

Please send me the items checked above. I am enclosing $_____.
(please add $1.00 to cover postage per order. OH add 6.25% tax. NJ add
6%). Send check or money order, no cash or C.O.D.s, please.
          To place a credit card order, call 1-800-847-8270.

NAME _____

ADDRESS _____

CITY/STATE_____ ZIP _____

Heart♥ng Presents
Love Stories Are Rated G!

That's for godly, gratifying, and of course, great! If you love a thrilling love story, but don't appreciate the sordidness of some popular paperback romances, **Heartsong Presents** is for you. In fact, **Heartsong Presents** is the *only inspirational romance book club*, the only one featuring love stories where Christian faith is the primary ingredient in a marriage relationship.

Sign up today to receive your first set of four, never before published Christian romances. Send no money now; you will receive a bill with the first shipment. You may cancel at any time without obligation, and if you aren't completely satisfied with any selection, you may return the books for an immediate refund!

Imagine. . .four new romances every four weeks—two historical, two contemporary—with men and women like you who long to meet the one God has chosen as the love of their lives. . .all for the low price of $9.97 postpaid.

To join, simply complete the coupon below and mail to the address provided. **Heartsong Presents** romances are rated G for another reason: They'll arrive *Godspeed!*